"Actually, I thought of a third option, and it's probably the best one yet.

"You could stay at my apartment and save us the trip back here as well as the expense of a hotel."

Annie's heart dipped. "That's nice of you, Mr. Brady, but I'm not in the habit of spending the night with strange men."

"I'm harmless, Anne. And call me Joe. We just dodged bullets and jumped off a fire escape together. In my book, that qualifies as bonding and the right to be on a first-name basis."

Annie laughed. And relaxed a little. This man could easily have left her to her own devices more than once tonight. Instead he'd risked his life to help her.

Annie thought she might be well hidden at Joe Brady's place, but she wasn't so sure she'd be "safe." His eyes were more than dark and unsettling. They looked honest, too. And friendly. And right now she needed a friend.

"Okay, I'll stay with you."

Jennifer Archer

As a frequent speaker at writing workshops, women's events and creative-writing classes, award-winning author Jennifer Archer enjoys inspiring others to set goals and pursue their dreams. She is the mother of two grown sons and currently resides in Texas with her high school sweetheart and their neurotic Brittany spaniel. Jennifer enjoys hearing from her readers through her Web site, www.jenniferarcher.net.

ANNIE on the LAM:
A Christmas Caper

Jennifer Archer

ANNIE ON THE LAM: A CHRISTMAS CAPER

copyright © 2007 by Jennifer Archer

i s b n - 1 3 : 9 7 8 - 0 - 3 7 3 - 8 8 1 4 8 - 2

i s b n - 1 0 :   0 - 3 7 3 - 8 8 1 4 8 - 7

TheNextNovel.com

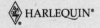 HARLEQUIN®

PRINTED IN U.S.A.

From the Author

Dear Reader,

Christmas is here! One of my favorite times of year. Family, decorated trees, twinkling lights, shiny wrapped packages, beloved carols. Unfortunately, all these wonderful things come with stress attached. Most women lead busy lives, and the holiday season only makes them busier. Sometimes in the middle of all the festivities we ladies could use a temporary escape.

With that in mind, I wrote *Annie on the Lam: A Christmas Caper*—a story quite different than any I've written before. Annie Macy, an aging Southern belle and the heroine of this story, needs to escape, too. But not from shopping and holiday cheer. Annie's running from the clutches of her overprotective daddy and the wrath of her criminal boss whose underhanded dealings she's determined to expose. So climb in the car and escape with Annie as she hits the road with a sexy P.I. who is working undercover as a cab driver. Sit back and hold on tight! I hope you enjoy the ride.

Merry Christmas and happy reading!

Jennifer Archer

Annie Macy studied her reflection in the full-length mirror and wondered what in the hell she was thinking when she let Aunt Tawney plan her wedding. Crisp white taffeta gowns and delicate lace veils were for twenty-something brides. Even a thirty-year-old would be pushing it to go to this extreme. But forty? Good gawd. She looked ridiculous. She looked desperate. Annie met her own gaze in the mirror. *She looked miserable.*

"Would you tilt your head a little to the left, Sugar?" her aunt asked in a tremulous voice.

Annie complied while trying to generate some enthusiasm for the event ahead. In forty minutes, she would be Mrs. Lance Holcomb and she wasn't sure how she felt about that.

Not anymore. Not after yesterday. *Before* that, if she were honest with herself.

Couldn't Tawney and everyone else buzzing about the dressing room see that she was only going through the motions, too confused to do anything else? Or were they all so caught up in the idea of happily-ever-after that they didn't notice?

Maybe they simply chose to ignore anything that might cause a hitch in The Plan—as in, get Annie married off before it's too late. She couldn't count the number of times over the last few years that Aunt Tawney had said a woman over forty had a better chance of getting struck by lightning than snagging a man. Tawney refused to hear Annie's reminders that *Time* or *Newsweek* or whichever publication had written that statement reneged on it later. Tawney believed it. Period.

Deep down, Annie had continued to buy into the dismal declaration, too. In her twenties, if someone had asked how she imagined her life would be at the age of forty, she would've said she'd have it all—a position of responsibility and power at her father's bank, a husband who was her equal, children.

She had none of those things.

Two years ago her biological clock had progressed from ticking to hammering away like a nervous woodpecker as the possibility of a husband and children slipped further and further out of her reach. Then her father hired Lance, introduced them to one another, and they hit it off. When Lance proposed one month before her fortieth birthday, the woodpecker took a breather and Annie shared its relief. She cared for Lance, they enjoyed each other's company. He was charming and funny, ambitious and interesting and smart. They were good together.

In addition to possibly making a beautiful baby, Annie

knew they would make a great business team, too. She spent a lot of time frustrated with her father for not giving her more responsibility at work, more free rein. Annie tried to be patient, to humor him. Milford Macy was from the old school, and though he exasperated her, she respected his dedication to the business he'd built. She might be his daughter, but she would have to work her way up, learn the ropes the hard way before stepping into his shoes. Annie had been doing just that since dropping out of college twenty years earlier, convinced she could learn more from her father than a textbook.

Luckily, Lance shared her vision for the bank. He listened to her ideas, offered opinions, insights and suggestions. Lance had never voiced any objections to being the man behind the woman some day when she inherited the controlling share of First Bank of Savannah. Not that she wanted that; she would be happy to have him as her equal partner.

Unless…

"This veil…" Aunt Tawney sighed. "It's not quite right." She stood on tiptoe, her stubby plump fingers smoothing and adjusting as they had for the past half hour.

Again Annie shifted her attention to the mirror, to the blur of rustling pale-pink behind her. At the vanity that stretched across the back wall, her University of Georgia sorority sisters from twenty years prior fussed with their makeup and hair. Two of them, anyway. Charlene Willoby Blackthorn and Reece Osborne Calhoun giggled, whispered and cooed like teenaged girls, their voices unnaturally giddy in the stuffy room. Only the maid of honor, Sara Buckhorn Miles, seemed unfazed by all the froufrou feminine folderol. Sara paced and smoked and shot Annie pointed glances every five seconds.

They look like perimenopausal poodles, Annie thought, feeling removed from the scene, as if she were watching her life play out on a television screen, a low-budget, groan-inducing movie of the week on the "horror" channel. In addition to Annie's dress, Aunt Tawney had chosen the frilly, silly, pastel bridesmaid gowns. The society page would have a heyday with this. By tomorrow morning, Annie figured she would be the laughingstock of Savannah, but she was too numb to care.

The door squeaked open. Annie's aunt Tess, the youngest of her father's sisters, stepped into the chaos. Sixty and long-divorced, Tess was as tall and svelte and bold as Tawney was short and plump and timid. "I just saw Lance." Grinning, she fanned her face, sending her own tobacco-laced scent adrift in the room. "My, oh my. You're one lucky girl, Annie-fo-fannie. That man is mouthwatering gorgeous in holey jeans. You'll drool like the village idiot when you see him in his tux."

Annie heard a swish of taffeta as Charlene stepped closer. Misty-eyed and gushing, she took Annie's hand and gave it a squeeze. "*Mr. and Mrs. Lance T. Holcomb.*" She sighed. "I'm so happy for you, honey. It's finally happening. After all these years."

"Happy for her? I'm proud of her," Reece huffed. "Unlike some of us, Annie held out for a bona fide catch."

Sara came up alongside Annie and in a quiet voice said, "Hey." Motioning with her head toward the door, she added, "You want to go for a walk?"

"Oh, my no," Tawney chirped. "Don't be silly. She doesn't have time for a walk." Wrinkling her nose and waving cigarette smoke away from Annie's gown with a fluttering hand, the older woman added, "Please put that nasty thing out, Sara. Today of all days, we don't want Annie to smell like an ashtray."

Annie kept her focus on Sara's knowing eyes. Those eyes saw things the others didn't. Those eyes would not allow Annie to fool herself. "I *could* use some air," she murmured. "Aunt Tawney, why don't you help Charlene and Reece finish up? We won't be long, I promise."

"Sugar…you'll mess up your gown."

"I'll hold the train for her," Sara said, then nudged Annie and murmured, "Let's go."

They hurried from the dressing room into its adjoining sitting area and out into the hallway, headed for the door that opened onto the church's side lawn. It was hotter than blazes outside, a typical sultry Georgia June. After only five seconds on the small porch, Annie started to perspire beneath all her layers of lace.

Sara reached into the bodice of her dress and pulled out a tiny silver flask. "Here. You look like you could use this."

"You know I don't drink hard stuff."

"Today's a good day to start."

Annie couldn't disagree. She plucked the flask from her friend's hand, twisted off the cap, took a swig, coughed and choked as it burned its way down.

"You don't have to do this," Sara said. "I can tell you're having second thoughts. What's wrong?"

Annie took another smaller sip of Southern Comfort before handing the flask back to Sara. "After the rehearsal last night…" She nibbled her lip.

"Tell me," Sara prodded.

Annie drew a steadying breath. "I'd left the church, but I forgot something so I came back. The only cars left in the parking lot were Lance's and Vivienne's."

"Vivienne? Your wedding planner?" When Annie nodded, Sara's eyes widened then narrowed. "I *knew* it." She jerked the flask up to her lips and tilted it back. "That *asshole*. What were they doing?"

"Nothing except talking inside the sanctuary. But he touched her arm and—" When tears threatened, Annie averted her gaze to a thick grove of trees at the far edge of the parking lot. "The way Lance looked at her…his body language…"

"What, Annie?" Sara asked softly.

"He never looks at *me* like that." Her voice faltered. "He doesn't smile at me that way or reach out and touch me…"

"Oh, honey." Sara offered the flask again.

Pressing her lips together, Annie shook her head and waved it away. Now that the words were spoken, the little whisper in her head that had warned her for months not to marry Lance grew louder. She had chosen not to listen to it before. Considering her history, she had chalked it up to staying single for so long and having cold feet when it came to marriage. Annie wasn't proud of the fact that she'd been engaged twice before and had broken off both relationships. But despite her growing reputation as a runaway bride, she couldn't ignore this whisper any longer. It was even more insistent than the ones from the past. "What should I do?" she squeaked and met Sara's gaze.

"What do you want to do?"

"My aunts...Daddy...they've gone to so much trouble and expense. And I've already backed out twice before."

Sara waved off her words. "Those didn't count. You called them off before anyone gave you so much as a butter dish. And you were a baby. You shouldn't have been thinking about marriage in the first place."

"I was twenty-five with Avery and thirty with Chuck."

"Thirty? Really?" Sara's wince was quick but not quick enough that Annie didn't see it. "I thought you were younger." She cleared her throat. "You did the right thing on both counts. Chuck's a workaholic and Avery can't get it up."

"Avery's impotent now? How do you know?"

"His ex has a big mouth."

Annie sighed. "My family thinks the world of Lance.

They won't understand. They think he's the perfect catch."
Everyone thought so.

Everyone except Sara.

"I'm not sure your wedding day is the appropriate time
for me to say this…" Sara hesitated, took another sip from
the flask. "On second thought, maybe it's the *perfect* time.
I don't understand why everyone can't see what he's been
up to from the beginning."

"What are you talking about?"

She laid a hand on Annie's arm. "Lance doesn't act like
a man who's in love, honey. I've always thought he was after
your dad's business holdings and going through you to get
them. If I were a betting woman, I'd place my money on
Lance Holcomb as a schemer and an opportunist. I thought
you'd see it eventually or I would've said something before
you agreed to marry him. After that, I was afraid of ruining
our friendship if I pointed it out."

Annie blanched. Then she had to speak. "You hinted.
And I did pick up on the clues that something wasn't right.
I just didn't want to believe it. I still don't. I can't believe
he'd use me. Lance isn't like that." Or was he? Honestly,
Annie wasn't sure. Sweat trickled down into her cleavage.
She fanned her face and chest with a hand. "So what if he
doesn't look at me in a certain way? Lance is *good* to me."

"Good isn't good enough. You deserve *great*." Sara tilted
her head to one side. "I'll ask you what I ask my girls
whenever they think they're in love. Does Lance wow you?"

"*Wow* me?" Annie thought about all that implied. She cared for Lance, was attracted to him, but did she love him? She wasn't even sure romantic love really existed. Not the kind you read about, the kind she had once believed in. Maybe caring for someone *was* love. "Did Craig wow you?" she asked Sara.

Sara's brows wiggled. "Did he ever. I remember the first time it hit me that I *had to have him*. I got this little *zing* in the pit of my stomach." She blushed beneath her scattering of freckles, then frowned at Annie's expression and added, "You don't have a clue what I'm talking about, do you?"

Annie didn't answer.

"That's what I was afraid of. If you'd felt that zing with Lance, you wouldn't have a single doubt in your mind about marrying him. Wild horses couldn't drag you away from the altar."

"But you were in your twenties when you married. Maybe a woman my age needs something different in a relationship. Something more stable…and respect."

"Stability and respect *are* important." Sara smiled. "But even though Craig's physique looks more like the Pillsbury Doughboy's these days than Matthew McConaughey's, he *still* wows me, and I still need it."

A knock sounded behind them, and Annie turned to see Aunt Tawney at the window, waving her in. She mouthed *okay* to her aunt, then said to Sara, "Today more than ever, I miss my mother. She was the perfect wife. She'd know what I should do." Annie scratched beneath the itchy veil and it tilted precariously to one side of her head. "I need time to think."

Sara glanced at her watch. "You'd better hurry." She screwed the cap onto the flask and returned it to her bodice.

Annie grimaced at the sight of carrot-top Sara in the pansy-pink bridesmaid gown. Despite hovering tears, she managed a small laugh. "You sure you're not warning me off Lance just so you won't have to walk down the aisle in that dress?"

"Lord." Sara shook her head and tugged at her neckline. "What was your aunt thinking?"

"She went a little overboard on the girly quotient."

"A little? This thing is gawd-awful."

Annie shrugged. "She and Tess only had sons. Tess couldn't care less about all this, but Tawney was so into the planning, I let her do her thing."

"Well, I'd wear the dress with a smile if you were marrying the right guy."

Straightening the pearl-studded bow centered between Sara's breasts, Annie blurted a laugh. "You *are* a good friend."

"Damn right I am." Sara winked, then they hooked arms and went inside.

On their way back to the dressing room, they spotted Charlene and Reece standing with Sara's husband at the opposite end of the hallway.

When Craig waved, Sara said, "I think I'll go join them." She squeezed Annie's hand. "Only you know what's right for you, honey. Not me or your family or anyone else. Make up your own mind about Lance. I'll be close by if you need me." Like a fluffy pink cloud, she floated off toward the others.

As Annie stepped into the sitting area adjoining the dressing room, her aunts' voices drifted to her. Something about Tawney's tone made her pause outside the slightly open door.

"Lord, please just let this be a case of the jitters and not another bail-out," Aunt Tawney said in a worried voice. "We'll give her a few minutes, then I'm going to drag her in here by the hair if I have to."

"I can't blame her. She's been single awhile," Tess replied. "Trust me, you get set in your ways when you live alone for a long time. If I were in her shoes, *I* wouldn't go through with it."

"But Annie's not like you. She needs someone to take care of her."

Flinching, Annie braced a hand against the wall. She needed someone to take care of her? Since when?

"I know you and Milford believe that," Tess said dryly, "But I'm not so sure. Annie's been taking care of herself just fine for years."

"Her *daddy* takes care of her," Tawney scoffed.

"In a way, I suppose. Milford certainly sees to it her life is carefree."

Anger bubbled up in Annie. Is that what everyone

thought? That she sat back and allowed her father to make her life easy and smooth? Yes, she had a hefty trust fund, but she also worked her butt off.

"And Annie *dropped out* of college, you may recall. She didn't just *leave*," Aunt Tawney went on. "Who can blame Milford for looking for someone to step in at the bank when he retires? In forty years, Annie has yet to commit to anything—college, two prior engagements. She can't be trusted to follow through. Why, in junior high, she even refused to finish charm school."

Humiliation as hot as the Georgia heat wrapped around Annie.

"*Charm school*," Tess huffed. "If I'd known dropping out was an option, I'd have turned tail when I was a girl, too. Who gives a damn about how to flutter your eyelashes? Not anybody I care to know. Maybe Annie's just smarter than the rest of us. She does things her own way."

"Exactly. She's always trying to push newfangled business ideas on Milford. I say if it ain't broke don't fix it. If she took over, I'm afraid to think what might happen."

"Milford should give her a chance, think a little less about the welfare of his precious bank and more about her."

"He *is* thinking about her. She'll get her inheritance whether or not she has control of it. He's only looking out for Annie by finding the right person to manage her interests. Milford won't be around forever to watch out for her. Thank God Lance came along. Our big brother can finally rest easy. Not only can Lance take care of the bank, he can take care of Annie in other ways, too."

"Now see, that's what bothers me. She's forty years old for gawd's sake. Why in the world is he so overprotective? She doesn't need watching over or to be taken care of." Tess sighed. "When Lydia died, he pressed his thumb on that girl and he hasn't lifted it since. I don't know how Annie has put up with it for so long."

"He lost the love of his life, Tess. He's terrified of losing her, too."

Even after twenty-four years, the mere mention of her mother's death brought painful memories back to Annie. To this day, she missed her. And her father…he'd been so fragile, so devastated after the accident. Annie had been sixteen at the time, and watching her father's heart break had almost killed her, too. She had understood that he over-protected her out of love and a pressing fear that she also might slip away from him. That's why she put up with his meddling long after she saw her first wrinkle in the mirror.

"The love of his life?" Tess made a hissing sound. "Lydia spent more time in New York City partying with her seedy friends that last year than she did with her own husband and child."

Annie jolted. She had to physically stop herself from stepping into the room and coming to her mother's defense. Her mom had been chairman of the Savannah chapter of Women For Women, a national charitable organization helping homeless women find shelter and work. The chapter was new and struggling to find its feet when her mother took office. Lydia had traveled to New York periodically that year to learn strategies from that city's more established chapter, not to party.

"And that lie about her charity work," Tess said with disgust. "Did she think he wouldn't find out she resigned her position almost before she began? From the start, I think her intention for taking it was to have a cover for those trips."

Unable to believe what she was hearing, Annie closed her eyes. A sick feeling settled in the pit of her stomach.

"Please, sister," Tawney said in a low tone. "This isn't the time to dig up family scandals. Thank God Milford was able to bury that particular one in the first place." Whispering now, she added, "No one knows that she wasn't alone in that car. Let's keep it that way."

Tess sighed again. "Milford's afraid Annie's like her, isn't he?"

"She *is* like her mother. So much so it's scary sometimes. She inherited Lydia's restless spirit, her inability to ever be satisfied and follow through with anything she starts. Milford's not about to let Annie spiral down and self-destruct like Lydia did."

Annie pressed a hand across her mouth and let their words sink in. Obviously there was more to her mom's death than she'd been told. More than a woman making too sharp a turn and going off a bridge on a rainy night while away in New York on volunteer business.

And if her aunts' implications were true, there was more to her mother than she had ever known, too.

"Annie's always had her head screwed on straight," Tess admonished. "She's not selfish. That's more than anyone can say about Lydia."

"Don't tell me you don't see her mother in her."

"In some ways, yes. She can be impulsive at times, and restless like you said, but—" Tess jerked her head toward the door, as if she heard something that alerted her of a presence on the other side.

Annie counted to five, then stepped in, noting their startled expressions.

"Well!" Tawney said and clapped her hands. "There's our girl. We were getting worried about you."

Beyond the door, the music changed to Pachelbel's "Canon in D," Annie's cue to leave for the sanctuary. She looked from one aunt to the other. If Tawney was right and her father was grooming Lance to take over the bank, she had only been fooling herself to think they would ever be equal partners. After they married, her life would be little more than that of a wealthy man's wife, one busy with chairing fund-raising benefits, entertaining her husband's clients, their friends. A life as a middle-aged Savannah socialite.

Her mother's life.

Is that what drove Lydia to her death? Had those trips to

New York been her attempt to escape a life that didn't fit her? In that moment, Annie longed to talk to her mother, to ask Lydia's advice and hear her side of the story. Had she once been as confused as Annie was now? Loving and wanting to please Milford, but needing something other than the life he offered? Had her mother felt trapped and unfilled and bored to tears?

"I need to talk to Lance," she said. She would ask him point-blank why he wanted to marry her, if he loved her, or if he only wanted her inheritance.

"But, Annie…" Tawney stepped toward her, reaching out a hand. "Vivienne will be here any minute."

"Chirping orders and fluttering about like a sparrow on speed, no doubt." Tess rolled her eyes and pulled a cigarette from the package in Sara's purse. "Some wedding planner. She's late." She met Annie's gaze and nodded at the door. "Go talk to Lance. I'll tell *Vivienne* to cool her jets."

Annie swung around and started from the room. Seconds later, at Lance's dressing-room door, she knocked once, then went in without an invitation.

Lance and Vivienne jumped apart, their eyes wide and startled. Vivienne tugged the hem of her dress down over her hips. Lance's hand flew up to his crooked bow tie.

Annie stared at them, waiting for a stab of pain that never came. She only felt a gnawing ache of humiliation and betrayal that swiftly transformed into disappointment before morphing into sadness. Then, just as quickly, relief swept through her. Lance had confirmed that her misgivings about marrying him were justified. She was doing the right thing by walking away. Sara had been right about him all along. He didn't give a whit about her; he only wanted the financial and career fringe benefits that their marriage would provide.

"I wasn't aware that that particular service was included in your fee," she said to Vivienne. Shifting her focus to Lance she added, "Or did you pay extra for it?"

"Annie…" His face flushed maroon.

"You two just made what I came here to say a whole lot easier." She pulled off the ridiculous, itchy veil, tossed it to Vivienne, scratched her head. "I don't want to marry you, Lance."

As "Trumpet Voluntary" began playing in the sanctuary, Annie turned and left without waiting for Lance to respond.

AT NOON the next day, Annie sat across a table from her Aunt Tess. Every noise in the café entered her ears and banged against her brain. "Thanks for coming," she said, spooning sugar into her tea.

Tess slipped off her reading glasses, set them aside along with the menu. "Are you hung over?"

"I wish. At least then I'd have some fun memories to go along with this headache." She stirred the tea. "I didn't sleep last night."

Tess's jaw clenched. "Firing Lance Holcomb isn't enough

punishment for what he did to you. And with the *wedding planner*. How cliché. Your father should've strangled him."

"Daddy fired Lance?" Annie sat straighter.

"Last night. You haven't talked to your father?"

"No." She hadn't picked up his calls. "I wanted to talk to you first. I guess I'm a little upset with him. A *lot* upset. And confused." Noticing Tess's baffled expression, she continued, "It wasn't what Lance did that kept me up last night. I was thinking about Mama."

Tess met her gaze, held it. "You heard Tawney and me talking, didn't you?" Without waiting for an answer, she slumped back against the chair, crossed her arms and sighed. "I'm sorry, Annie."

"Daddy's been lying to me, hasn't he? All these years."

"No, Annie, not lying, really. Just—"

"Not telling the whole truth."

"You were so young when the accident happened. He wanted to spare you more pain."

"I'm not young now. I haven't been for years." She stared across at her aunt. "Was my mother having an affair?"

Tess bowed her head and pinched the bridge of her nose. "Lord. You should ask your father these questions."

"I'm asking you. You and I have never played games with each other. Let's not start now."

Tess looked up and said, "I don't know if she was having an affair. That's the truth."

"Aunt Tawney said there was someone in the car with her

when it crashed. Was it a man?" Tess's silence was all the answer she needed. Annie studied the older woman's nervous expression for a minute as a multitude of unnamed emotions twisted and tangled inside her. Finally, she asked, "Who was he?"

"Digging all this up won't bring your mother back. It won't change anything."

"*I need to know.*" Annie leaned in across the table. "I'm forty years old and suddenly I realize I don't even know who my mother was, who *I* am or what I want to do with the rest of my life. I feel like I've wasted so many years." She covered her aunt's wrinkled hand with her own on the tabletop. "Aunt Tawney said I'm like her. So did you. Apparently my father thinks so, too. And that frightens him enough that he's been desperate to find someone to act as my watchdog before he has to give up the duty."

"That's not how it is, Annie."

"That *is* how it is. It occurred to me last night that Daddy introduced me to all three men I've been engaged to."

Tess bent her head and stared down at her lap.

"I'm the same age she was when she died, do you realize that? Maybe if I understood—" Her throat closed and she looked away.

"Okay." Tess glanced up, wariness in her eyes. "You are like Lydia in a lot of ways. But you're different, too. You're your own person. Understanding your mother isn't necessarily the key to understanding yourself."

"But it might be. I need the truth. Why was my mother traveling to New York? I know she wasn't doing charity work."

Tess stared at her a minute then said, "Lydia was bored. At first she did go for the charity, then she resigned her position, but we didn't know that for a while. Judging by the little your father was able to learn after the accident, we think she might've been trying to set things up so that she could move there."

"You mean leave Daddy."

"Yes."

"And me."

"I can't answer that. Nobody can. Your father did some investigating and found out she'd invested most of her inheritance she hadn't already squandered in some sort of business venture that never played out."

Sadness swam through Annie. "When I think about her...she seemed withdrawn and tired a lot of the time. And not only that last year. I didn't dwell on it much then. But looking back now that I'm older, I can't help wondering if she was depressed because she hated her life here."

"Lydia did see a doctor for depression. She had trouble sleeping. But knowing her, I'm not sure she would've been any happier doing anything else, *anywhere* else."

Annie didn't want to believe that. She wanted to believe that her family was wrong about her mother, that they simply had not understood her. "The man in the car...you didn't tell me his name."

Tess closed her eyes briefly. Said, "Milford's going to kill me." Sighed. "His name was Fred or Frank…Reno. Something like that. Your father had him checked out afterward. He was just some flashy, loud-mouthed loser who owned a club or two in the city. I can't imagine what Lydia was doing getting mixed up with someone like him, but we found out he's the person she invested the money with."

"You said 'was'. Did he die, too?"

"No, he survived. With little more than a few scratches, actually. It was his car, by the way. Your mother was driving and he was in the passenger seat. We don't know why."

"Did Daddy confront him?"

"No. What good would it do? It wouldn't bring Lydia back. And, honestly, I think he was afraid of finding out something about her he didn't want to know." Tess leaned in across the table. "Whatever you're thinking, Annie, let it drop. You might not want to know, either." Blinking, Tess scanned the café and said, "What's taking our waitress so long?"

Noting her aunt's escalating nervousness, Annie said, "There's something else, isn't there?"

After a long stretch of silence, Tess blinked at her, released a long breath and said, "It's only speculation, but after talking with several witnesses to the accident, the authorities thought Lydia might've driven off the bridge on purpose."

CHAPTER 2

Six months later
December, New York City

Unwrapping his meatball sandwich, Joe Brady stepped out of the deli and crossed to the curb. A bite on the run was his usual routine these days. In that respect, driving a cab for a living was not so different than being a cop.

Weather reports predicted a blizzard on the way. Bitter gray cold had arrived ahead of the snow. Joe shivered as he slid behind the wheel. His cell phone rang and he leaned back to pull it from the front pocket of his jeans, noticing that the charge was low. He couldn't seem to remember to plug the damn thing in when he had the chance.

"Brady, here," he said, around a mouthful of beef.

"Hey, Joe. Ed Simms."

"Ed! Good to hear your voice." The old guy had been on the force with Joe's father Patrick back in the day. As a kid, Joe had spent many an hour with the Simms family. Later, Ed had opened his own private investigation firm and it had thrived. Word was, he'd retired with a nice little nest egg. In Joe's opinion, it couldn't have happened to a nicer guy. "Where you been keepin' yourself, buddy?"

"Out of trouble. Old age agrees with me."

Joe chuckled. "How's Nancy?"

"Doin' good, doin' good. She loves living out of the city. And she's enjoying the grandkids. You should come see 'em sometime. Bring your mother. Have dinner."

"She'd like that. So would I." In fact, his mother would like living out of the city, too.

"How is she, anyhow?"

"Good. She misses Pop, but she's learning to be happy alone." By driving Joe crazy, but he wouldn't share that with Ed. "It's almost two years Pop's been gone now."

"Hard to believe. I miss him, too," Ed murmured. "How about you? Still driving a cab?"

"Part-time between cases."

After a short pause, the older man said, "I still say you were too hard on yourself after all that mess went down. You're a detective, not a P.I. Or a cabbie, for that matter. But it's good to know you're staying busy."

"I could be busier," Joe admitted. He placed the messy sandwich on the seat beside him and stuck his key into the ignition. He hadn't heard from Ed in months and wondered what had prompted this particular call. More than an offhand dinner invitation and a subtle lecture, he guessed. "What's up, Ed?"

"I had a call today from an old client. Hotshot banker from Savannah name of Milford Macy. His old lady drove a car off a bridge into the Hudson more than twenty years ago and he hired me to check out the vehicle's owner, a fellow who was riding along in the passenger seat. I believe you know the guy."

"Oh, yeah?" Joe checked the traffic over his shoulder and prepared to merge into it.

"It was Frank Reno."

Slamming his foot down on the brake, he threw the cab into Park and stayed put. "No shit."

"I thought that might get your attention."

"You thought right."

"Anyhow, I didn't find out much at the time. Just that Macy's wife and Reno were doing some kind of business together. He was small-time back then, but already threatening enough that if anybody knew anything they weren't willing to talk. I advised Macy to let it drop and go on with his life, and that's what he did after taking some steps to keep the details of the accident low-profile. Didn't want the scandal of a possible suicide reaching the tea sippers back home in Georgia."

"So why's he calling you again after so long?"

"Seems his daughter moved to the city last summer and went to work at a bank. No big deal until a couple of months go by and she takes on a second job working as a waitress at Landau's."

"I know the place," Joe said.

"You know Harry Landau?"

"I know of him. He's Reno's nephew."

"That's right. Reno set him up in the restaurant business. Macy didn't make the connection but a little red flag went up when his kid started calling home with a lot of vague questions about money laundering, etcetera, etcetera. He was afraid she might've gotten herself in the middle of something way out of her league."

"Takes after her mother, huh?"

"Apparently. So he calls me this morning and asks me if I'd check out Harry Landau, and when I tell him Landau's bad news, that he's Reno's nephew, and then bring him up to date on Reno's activities in the years since his wife bought it in that car—"

"Damn. Did he wet his pants?"

"The poor guy was pretty shook up. Now he's thinking it's no coincidence that his kid landed herself a job at Landau's. He thinks she's up to something, and I tend to agree with him."

"Man." Joe shook his head, reached for his sandwich, put it down again. He'd lost his appetite. Frank Reno was directly related to his reasons for turning in his badge a year ago. Joe was no longer a police detective, but he still wanted the son-of-a-bitch's head on a plate more than just about anything.

"Macy wants someone to keep an eye on his daughter for a while. I told him I'm out of the business, but that I knew an ex-cop familiar with Reno—that'd be you—and that you have a real hard-on for the guy."

Joe winced at Ed's choice of words. "Actually it's nailing him to the wall that excites me," he said caustically, "Not the man himself."

Ed chuckled. "You in? He's willing to pay out the nose." The old man quoted a daily rate that shot Joe's pulse through the roof.

He took about five seconds to think it over. Joe didn't like the idea of babysitting some socialite who was probably playing with fire just to add a little excitement to her life, but he needed the cash. And he couldn't bring himself to pass up an opportunity that carried even a slim chance of taking him one step closer to locking Reno away where he belonged.

He picked up his sandwich again and a meatball rolled into his lap. Frowning at the red smear of sauce on his jeans, Joe said, "Give me Macy's number. I'll give him a call. And thanks, Ed."

THE FOLLOWING NIGHT, Joe sat in the cab on a side street with the headlights off and his eye out for the cops since he'd parked by a pump. The last thing he needed right now was a ticket and he wasn't counting on any special treatment, ex-detective or not.

He adjusted his iPod earplugs and hit play. Music pulsed through his head. If AC/DC couldn't keep him awake, nothing could. Anticipating at least another boring hour or two ahead, he settled back to watch the falling snow and the traffic at 32nd and Park.

Even at midnight, the windows of the high-rise building across the street blazed like a blowtorch and the trees lining the sidewalks twinkled with tiny white Christmas lights. Beside those trees, people still strolled, some pausing to admire holiday displays behind the glass storefronts: figurines and trains and miniature villages.

Joe yawned. New York City might function just fine without sleep, but he didn't. He longed for his nice warm bed and at least eight hours of peace and quiet.

Trailing his gaze from Landau's on the top floor of the building down to the street-level entrance, he tapped his fingers on the steering wheel to the beat of "Back In Black" then shivered and cursed. He wasn't sure if his ass was frozen or just paralyzed from boredom. Either way, he guessed he deserved a numb butt if he couldn't come up with a better way to earn a dollar.

Joe twisted his head side to side to work the kinks from his neck. He reached for the months-old newspaper on the seat beside him, pulled a penlight from his jeans pocket and clicked it on, illuminating an old issue of the *Savannah News* society page his newest client had sent to him by overnight FedEx. After skimming the full-color photo of the smiling blond socialite and her tuxedoed escort, Joe read the print beneath it: *Annabelle Macy and Mr. Lance Holcomb celebrate the announcement of their engagement at the home of Mr. Milford Macy...*

He returned his attention to the porcelain-doll blonde, a woman so elegant and fragile and hands-off perfect she looked like she'd shatter into a million jagged pieces if a man touched her. Her mouth might be smiling, but her eyes looked as bored and weary as he felt right now. Despite the enormous rock on her finger, the socialite looked unhappy. But what did he know about women? Especially rich ones? For all he knew, she might be upset that the rock wasn't bigger.

Joe skimmed a fingertip across Annabelle Macy's image. She was older than he had imagined, though her eyes looked like a lost little girl's.

He laughed at himself.

She was no little girl. Annabelle Macy would be a fine-looking woman even without all the jewels and fancy duds. But something other than her appearance drew his interest. Something in her expression, in her body language, made him sense more to this particular socialite than sparkle and shine. He thought he recognized the look of desperation on her face. It was the same one he saw in the mirror each morning. On an ex-cop, chewed up and spit out at the age of forty-one, he could understand and accept it. But what would cause a woman like Miss Macy to wear such a look? That mess with her mother? Even after twenty-four years? He didn't get it.

Joe studied the photo more closely and decided the look was probably boredom rather than desperation. The Macys had named their daughter well. Anna-*belle*. Rich, pampered, southern. Lacking nothing, but wanting more. He'd heard about her type. It was a long shot that he would gain any useful inside scoop regarding Reno by following her. In fact, the more he thought about it, the more he figured the chances were about as slim as his wallet. More than likely, Miss Macy was only playing mind games with her daddy, trying to get his dander up by going to work for Landau.

Joe snorted and laid the paper aside. The woman was old enough to have grown kids of her own. Some people just never grew up; some people didn't have to. Too bad he wasn't one of 'em.

When a knock sounded on the cab's passenger side, Joe jumped and dropped the penlight into his lap. Pulling out his earplugs, he turned and saw his cousin Dino at the window.

Dino opened the door and slid in. "Using my cab as an office, eh?"

"I finished my shift." When Dino opened his mouth to speak again, Joe added, "Look, I just need it a couple more hours. I pay for the gas, so what do you care?"

Dino sat back. Shivering, he tugged the side of his stocking cap down over one exposed ear. "Cold as a witch's tit out there."

Joe glanced back at the building. "I wouldn't know about that."

"You got hot water in your veins or somethin'?"

"Nope. Just never touched a witch's tit."

Chuckling, Dino rubbed his hands together to generate heat. "Finally got a case, huh?"

Joe twisted his neck until it popped and a dull ache spread up to his left temple. "Yeah. Yesterday."

"How many does that make now? Three? Four?"

"Five." He squinted at his cousin. "What's it to you?"

Dino lifted his hands. "I don't mean nothing. Five's not bad. Better than a poke in the eye, ya know? You've only had your shingle out a year." He returned his hands to his lap. "Ever think of going back on the force?"

Scanning the cab's dismal interior, Joe smirked. "What? And give up all this? I'll stick with my five cases." *And driving your shit-hole of a cab part-time to make ends meet.* He drew a deep breath of cold, stale air tainted by years of spilled drinks and cigarette smoke.

For at least a minute, they stared in silence out the window. Then Dino reached across and lifted the newspaper from the seat. He glanced down at the photograph. "You tailing one of these?"

"The woman."

Dino's whistle was long and quiet. "She's a looker. What did she do?"

"You're nosy as hell, you know that?"

"Yeah…so, what'd she do?"

"Nothing unless you count leaving Georgia to move to the big city a crime."

"Who hired you?" Dino thumped the picture of Lance Holcomb. "This guy?"

"No, her father."

Dino drew back, lifted the paper closer to his face and narrowed his eyes. "She's a little long in the tooth to be answering to her daddy, ain't she?"

"Not in their world, I guess." Joe gave his cousin the short version of why Milford Macy had hired him.

Dino whistled again. "Reno, huh? You got a reason besides money for taking this case, then. Hope it works out for ya." He took a last look at the paper, chuckled and returned it to the seat. "Maybe she likes to stir things up to keep from gettin' bored. She's either gutsy or stupid."

"*Daddy* didn't give me the impression he thinks she's brave." Joe recalled the note of genuine distress and frustration in Milford P. Macy's voice. "He says she's impulsive." He paused a beat. "And in over her head."

"Is she?"

"What do *you* think? The woman works at a bank during the day and waits tables at Landau's at night."

"A rich broad like that?" Dino scoffed. "Why does she need to work at all?"

Joe thought about his phone conversations with her father. The fact that there was tension between the old man and his daughter had come across the line loud and clear.

"Milford Macy pulled some mighty big strings back in the eighties to keep the details surrounding his wife's demise hushed up," Joe told his cousin. "Didn't even tell Miss Annabelle the whole truth. But she found out recently, and I'm bettin' she wasn't too happy about being kept in the dark all these years. The job with Landau is probably her warped idea of payback."

"Funny way of gettin' back at her father, if you ask me." Dino looked out the window and up toward the building's top floor. "You ever met Harry?"

"Can't say I've ever had the pleasure," Joe answered sarcastically.

But Landau's name had come up more than once over the past year in his own personal private investigation of Frank Reno's many business endeavors. Reno headed up one of the city's most profitable drug rings. Everyone knew it. No one could prove it. Yet.

Dino laughed and shook his head. "I went to school with Harry. The guy dresses like a pimp. Did all right for himself, though. Legally or not, I couldn't say. But I hear the restaurant's classy. Wouldn't know personally." He sniffed and nodded at Joe. "The place is too uptown for our blood."

"Speak for yourself," Joe said, and smiled. "What makes you think I can't afford Landau's?"

Grinning, Dino answered, "Oh, yeah, that's right. I forgot about those five cases of yours." He shifted his long wiry frame, shivered and reached for the door handle. "Your mama's been calling mine worried about you."

"Tell Aunt Sophie to tell her I'm good."

"Maybe you oughta tell her."

"I have." Every time she called. Which was daily.

"Maybe Aunt Sophie will have better luck convincing her than I have."

Dino gave Joe's shoulder a soft punch. "You know my mama would never lie to her sister."

"I'm good," Joe repeated, averting his gaze to the newspaper in the seat. He heard the passenger door open, felt the frigid blast of air from outside, sensed Dino sliding out.

"No high-speed chases in my cab, understand?" his cousin teased.

"I'll try to keep it down to ninety." Joe smiled but didn't look up. "And speaking of your cab, the radio's on the fritz again. Never know if it's gonna work or not."

"I'll check it out tomorrow."

When the door slammed, Joe slipped the plugs back into his ears. He decided he should pay his mother a visit soon, cajole her into cooking his favorite meal, tease her about her new neighbor, Mr. Manning, until she blushed and laughed and shooed him out of her apartment. He didn't like her worrying about him. And he didn't like worrying about her. He had exaggerated to Ed Simms about her state of mind since his father's death. She was lonely. And Joe didn't like her living in the old neighborhood alone. All their close neighbors who had been there when he was growing up had either died or moved, and with the exception of Mr. Manning, the remaining tenants were not the sort he wanted his mother around. Joe wanted to help her move someplace safer, but she wouldn't hear of it until he had a "real" job again. One with steady pay.

He tapped his finger against the *Savannah News* and thought again that he had probably made a big mistake taking this case. Sure, the money was great, and he could put it to good use. But his gut told him that whether Miss Macy was in over her head or not, her daddy was being overly protective of a middle-aged daughter who wanted out from under his thumb. Macy probably really wanted a bodyguard for Miss Annabelle, not just a watchful pair of eyes.

After turning in his badge, Joe had promised himself he'd never again take on the responsibility of another person's safety. Especially if that person was female. The idea of breaking that promise, even for another possible chance at Reno, bothered him.

With one last glance at Annie Macy's photo, he folded the paper. *Damn those eyes.*

CHAPTER 3

Raucous laughter and strains of "Jingle Bell Rock" drifted down the hallway outside Harry Landau's dark office. Landau's Christmas party was at full drunken tilt.

Standing before an open file cabinet, Annie fought an oncoming sneeze. She wasn't sure whose Christmas gift was worse—Harry's perfume or the one his sister Lacy had given her. Lacy might not be the sharpest pencil in the box but she understood sarcasm; the woman knew condoms would be wasted on Annie. Lacy often teased her that if she didn't accept a date soon, she'd quality as a virgin again. The woman had a warped sense of humor.

Beyond the wall of office windows, Manhattan sparkled like a trimmed Christmas tree dusted with snow. Flakes danced in the night sky, the beginning of the blizzard the weather reports had predicted.

With trembling fingers, Annie pulled folders from the cabinet drawer and placed them into the empty briefcase she'd found in Harry's closet. Her heart pounded hard as she glanced over her shoulder at the closed door. She would've come more prepared, brought her own bag to haul all this stuff away in, but until Harry cornered her a few minutes ago, she had only intended to do some nosing around, not take anything. Not yet.

But now she knew she wouldn't be coming back. Risky or not, this was her last chance. When she walked out of Landau's for the last time, she would carry proof that Harry was laundering money through the restaurant. And she'd bet every dime of her inheritance that the proof would implicate Frank Reno, too.

Frank Reno. Annie bit down on her lip. She'd yet to meet the man, but she hated him. Over the past months, she'd scanned every newspaper and magazine article she could find on Reno, old and new. He'd made quite a name for himself over the past twenty-four years, rising to the top of New York's criminal who's-who. Yet, no matter the crime, he always managed to walk away scot-free. Just like he had after cheating her mother.

Not this time. Not if she could help it.

Before leaving Georgia to move to New York, Annie had visited the woman who had been her mother's best friend since childhood. When pressed, Barbara Tyler admitted that Lydia had confided in her about her intentions to leave Annie's father and move to New York upon firming up plans to open a restaurant. After that confession, Lydia's contact with Barbara became less frequent, so Barbara knew little else. But she did remember the name of a woman in New York Lydia had stayed with on more than one occasion.

It took some searching, but after arriving in New York City herself, Annie finally found Karla Wilshire in a hospice dying of cancer. Her mother's old acquaintance told her that she'd stayed quiet for years due to her fear of Frank Reno. But she had nothing to lose now, and she was willing to talk.

Karla said that Lydia had met Reno through a mutual friend. When Reno learned that Lydia wanted to move to the city, he offered her an investment opportunity in a restaurant he planned to open. Lydia came through with her end of the bargain; she gave him a chunk of money. And Reno ran with it. Literally.

Karla was with Annie's mother in the hours preceding her death. They'd gone out to a club with friends and ran into Reno. Lydia and Reno argued, and the club manager asked them to take it outside. Barbara watched them exit the front door, thinking they'd have their say and Lydia would return. But Annie's mother never came back. Karla didn't have any idea why Lydia might've left with Reno in his car, but she figured Annie's mom had insisted on driving because Frank was "flying higher than a kite" that night.

Thinking about that gave Annie the courage she'd needed to break into Harry's office. She blamed Frank Reno for her mother's death. Whether directly or indirectly, he was responsible; nobody could convince her otherwise. For whatever reasons, her mother had been troubled and desperate, and Frank Reno had taken advantage of that fact.

She closed one file drawer and opened another. Her nose twitched, her eyelashes quivered, her lips trembled as she tried to hold in the sneeze. What had she been thinking when she tested that perfume? She had inherited Aunt Tess's unladylike sneeze—a fact that had occasionally caused her some embarrassment, but until now, never anything life-threatening. Harry would kill her if he found her in here.

Annie continued dumping files into the briefcase. How could she have been so completely wrong about Harry? Everything about him seemed to indicate his sexual preference leaned toward the male gender. But that wasn't her only misconception. From the moment she met him up until the past couple of weeks, she had decided that if he was crooked, he must be the most mannerly criminal in the city. In the beginning, Harry was always friendly. Always polite. He could be charming and witty. She had applied for the waitressing job hoping she might meet his uncle Frank face to face. But after her first interview with Harry, she had assumed that he had not inherited any of his uncle's sleazy genes.

So much for assumptions.

When she'd overheard one of Harry's private conversations two weeks ago, her suspicions had flared. Seeing him shove Lacy and threaten her to keep quiet had inspired Annie to investigate those suspicions. But tonight was the only shove *she'd* needed to muster her courage and take action, to expedite and follow through on her plan.

Annie's hands shook as she slipped the last folder into Harry's briefcase, then closed and latched it. She set it on his desk and reached for her purse on the floor, placing her beaded bag beside the briefcase. She told herself that when this was all over, she needed to work on her perception skills involving men. When Harry Landau had found her alone in the hallway twenty minutes ago, she learned three truths about him. One: women's bodies ranked high on his list of interests; two: mature handling of rejection was not one of his strengths; and three: Harry wasn't fond of eggnog. At least not as a face cream. Recalling the fury in his eyes, Annie shuddered.

A second sneeze threatened. Closing her eyes, she drew in spasmodic breaths. She grabbed the briefcase handle with one hand while clamping her other hand across her mouth. Pinching her nostrils between her forefinger and thumb, she tried to muffle what she knew was to come. No luck. She succumbed.

Seconds after the sneeze, footsteps sounded in the hallway. The doorknob rattled. The lights in the office flashed on.

Briefcase in hand, Annie whirled around, knocking her purse off Harry's desk, scattering lipsticks and loose change, a hairbrush and compact, her cell phone and condoms…lots and lots of Lacy's Christmas gift condoms…across the leopard-print silk rug.

Harry stepped into the room. All five foot six inches, one hundred and forty lean, spidery pounds of him. In his tailored gold Christmas-party suit, green tie and red Santa hat, he looked too pretty to be male, too festive to be a crook, too silly to take seriously. Then his eyes narrowed.

"What in the hell are you doing in here?" he growled.

Annie slowly backed up until she bumped against the credenza behind Harry's desk. "I—" She swallowed. "I was just leaving."

"Why are you wearing my coat?"

She'd been trying to think smart, to plan ahead, when she'd slipped on the long fur parka she'd found draped across Harry's chair. It was freezing outside and she didn't know if she'd have to hoof it when she left here or if she'd be able to flag down a cab. Her own wrap was down the hall and she had not wanted to chance going back for it and running into Harry again. Since she was borrowing Harry's financial information, she'd decided she might as well help herself to his coat, too.

Taking the briefcase with her, she stooped to scoop everything back into her purse. But she'd only managed to retrieve her small leather journal and a few other items from the floor before the tips of Harry's buffed shoes appeared in her field of vision. Annie glanced up.

Harry's gaze took in the strewn condom packets before settling on her face. He grinned. "Changed your mind, did you?" He shifted his attention to the case in her hand and the grin disappeared. His smooth, pointed chin jutted out like a dagger, sharp and firm and uncompromising. "What are you up to?"

Crushing her purse against her stomach with her free hand, Annie stood, then darted for the opposite side of the desk—her only clear pathway to the door.

Harry grabbed a fistful of her hair and tugged. "That's my briefcase, you bi—"

Annie swung the case across her body, over her shoulder. It connected with something solid—Harry's mouth, she supposed, since a strangled grunt replaced his words. He released her hair and she turned and hit him again.

Harry reached between the lapels of the coat and grabbed the scooped neckline of her satin blouse. She heard a rip, felt the fabric give way. His nail scraped her skin. He slammed her against the credenza, wrapped his long slender fingers around her neck and squeezed.

Pressure filled Annie's head, panic fluttered in her chest. She tried to gasp but couldn't find any air. Channeling all her fear and adrenaline into the movement, she jammed her knee up hard into Harry's groin.

Harry recoiled.

Annie ran.

JOE'S HEAD ACHED and his eyelids sagged as he stared at the lobby door of the building across the street. When it swung open, he sat up straight.

A woman ran out, wobbling on classy high-heeled boots. She wore a long fur coat, clutched a purse in one hand, a briefcase in the other. Wind blew long blond hair across her face. Car horns blared and tires screeched as she darted across the street. Caught in a blur of headlights and swirling snow, she dodged and staggered but kept on moving.

Joe tugged the iPod plugs from his ears and tossed them aside. She was headed straight for him. He started the engine.

Behind the blonde at the building's entrance, a skinny little man in a garish gold suit and a Santa hat stumbled through the same door she'd exited. Doubled over, the man paused for a beat, looked left then right then into the street. Spotting the woman, he yelled something and pursued, one hand covering his crotch.

Joe rolled his window down. "Hey!" he shouted to the blonde as he threw the cab into gear. "Get in!"

She crammed her purse under her arm, almost tore the back door from the hinges, slid inside, shut it.

Mere seconds later, Santa reached the back window and slammed his fist against the glass.

Joe hit the locks.

"*Go!*" the woman shrieked as her pursuer shouted obscenities and continued to pummel the rear windshield. "*Go, go, get out of here. Hurry!*"

Joe jammed his foot down on the accelerator. The cab shot away from the curb. Tires squealed and horns blasted as he swerved into traffic. When they were a safe distance away, he glanced into the rearview mirror. The little guy in the gold suit stood at the edge of the street, one fist raised high, the other still guarding his crotch.

The woman turned and looked back, too.

"Friend of yours?" Joe asked, not bothering to hide the sarcasm in his voice.

"Boss," the lady said, then turned back around. For several moments, her fast, staggered breaths were the only sounds in the cab.

"You show up late for work, or what?"

"You might say I cleaned up his office a little." A short hysteria-laced laugh sounded from the back seat. "How was I supposed to know he likes things dirty?"

Thanks to the quick dose of adrenaline their fast get-away had shot into his bloodstream, Joe was wide-awake now, but his head pounded even worse than before. He drew a long, deep, nerve-settling breath.

City lights reflected off the snow, illuminating the cab's interior. Stopping at a red light, he cast a quick peek over one shoulder at his passenger. Her briefcase lay in her lap, her purse on the seat beside her. She gripped the case with one hand, the edge of the seat with the other as she twisted again to look out the back window.

"Relax. He's long gone," Joe said. He didn't require a second inspection of the photograph on the folded news-paper beside him to know that the woman in his back seat was the socialite he'd been hired to follow. Annabelle

Macy—Annie, her father had called her. Heiress from one of the wealthiest families in the state of Georgia. Hell, probably in the nation. Owner of that pair of troubled eyes that had haunted him all day. He opened the glove box, slipped the newspaper inside, latched it again.

Her slow drawl had caught him off guard, though he wasn't sure why. The money-dripping accent only confirmed what he'd suspected when he saw the newspaper photo. She sounded like she spent her days sitting on a plantation porch, sipping mint juleps and fanning her face while a staff of servants hovered around her.

Joe felt a sneer coming on. He had no patience for simpering Junior League types who fainted away when things got too hot. He should be shot for taking this case. He had better things to do than babysit a reckless, flighty, full-grown woman who liked to play games. Like take three aspirin and bury his throbbing head beneath a pillow.

Joe faced the street again. The light turned green. He started across the intersection, then adjusted the rearview mirror and caught another glimpse of his back seat passenger. *Whoa.* Full-grown was right. Miss Macy had turned away from the rear window. Her coat had fallen off one shoulder; the blouse beneath was torn, revealing the lacy top edge of a black bra and a nasty red scratch on the smooth swell of breast just above it. She slid down in the seat far enough to rest her head against it, closed her eyes. Wind-blown hair swept her shoulders in pale waves.

Well. Well. Things were definitely looking up. One glance at her had managed to do what his heavy leather jacket had failed to accomplish all night. Joe turned the heater down a notch. Where was the pretty, reserved ice princess from the newspaper? He smiled to himself. This lousy job came with a couple of perks. Who knew? Whether it led to Reno or not, maybe he *could* bear this side trip away from his usual routine. At least the scenery was nice. And a whole lot wilder than he'd expected.

A subtle scent of perfume drifted up to him; he heard each fast, erratic breath she drew. Joe thought over what she'd said about Harry Landau liking things "dirty." Now that was a loaded statement. He wondered if he could coax Miss Magnolia Blossom to talk, to narrow down the options for him. It wouldn't be easy. He doubted she'd willingly open up to a cab driver.

"Where to?" he asked, and she recited an address, *her* address. The one Milford Macy had given him over the phone. Joe had driven by a few times today.

"No, wait." She bolted upright in the seat. "Don't go there. Not yet. Just drive around."

He peeked at her again. She was staring out the window, worried eyes blinking, pretty brows puckered. Wincing, she shifted and looked down at the scratch on her breast then licked a fingertip and wiped away a smear of blood. Joe's pulse jumped, and when her eyes met his and narrowed, he jumped, too.

Glaring at him, she jerked the coat across her chest. "Do you mind?"

Not at all, Joe thought and looked back at the road just in time to slam on the brake and miss ramming the car ahead of them. His knee hit the underside of the steering column and he cursed, then muttered, "Sorry."

Turning the heater down another notch, he shifted lanes to pass the slow-moving car ahead of him. Boy, did this one have her daddy fooled. Milford Macy had painted a picture of his daughter as a naïve innocent.

Yeah right. And Joe was Pope Benedict.

He reminded himself he worked for Milford Macy, which meant *hands off. Don't even think about it.* But as long as he looked at Annabelle Macy, there was little chance he could think of anything else. She looked like sex, and he hadn't had any in so long he wasn't sure he'd remember how. He readjusted the mirror so he couldn't see her reflection without straining his neck.

"There's a police station around the next corner," he said.

"Police? I don't need the police."

"After that little incident with Santa I thought you might be in some kind of trouble." He tried to resist his impulses, failed, craned his neck to see into the mirror.

"I'm not in trouble." She tugged the briefcase closer to her body, looked down at it, met his gaze in the mirror.

"Are you sure about that?" he asked, wondering what was in that case.

"It's really none of your business, is it? I'm paying you to drive, not ask me twenty questions or give me advice."

The sneer returned. His head pounded harder. So did his knee. She might look good, but the woman was a spoiled witch with a capital *B*. "It's my *business* if you've made me an accomplice to something illegal. Like *theft*, maybe?"

"You're the one who pulled up and told me to get in."

"You want to tell me what's in that briefcase?"

"No, I don't. Do you always butt into the personal affairs of your passengers?"

Snooty-ass brat. Joe pressed down on the accelerator and picked up speed. If she wouldn't wise up and go to the police about whatever monkey business she was up to, maybe he'd just bring the cops to her. "Lady, I'm pretty sure I saved your prissy butt back there."

"You have a lot of nerve speaking to me like that."

"Your boss looked to me like he was ready to strangle you. If I were you—"

"Well, you *aren't* me." She reached up and braced her hands against the headrest in front of her. "Slow down. You're going to get us killed. In fact, pull over at that coffee shop. I want out."

Joe whipped to the curb alongside a meter and screeched to a stop. *Good riddance*, he thought, then *damn*. Nothing would please him more than to say so long to Miss Sweet Tea. Nothing except the big fat wad of money her daddy owed him if he stuck this out for the next few days. And then there was the chance of finding out something about Reno he could use, though he'd pretty much written off that possibility.

Joe drew a breath, another, then asked, "Do you want me to wait?"

"No, thanks. I've had all the fun I can stand. How much do I owe you?"

She didn't owe him a dime since Daddy was footing the bill. Still, Joe looked at the meter and quoted her a price.

With a sigh, she opened her purse, her head down. "Thank you," she muttered in a grudging tone. "You did save my butt, as you so crudely pointed out. But it's *not* prissy."

Prove it, Joe thought, wishing she would ditch that huge piece of animal hide she wore so he could decide for himself. He reined in that thought before it could turn into a full-fledged fantasy.

"I know you probably think I'm rude," she continued, digging through the purse now. "I'm not. Not usually, anyway. It's just that I'm sick and tired of people telling me what I should do." She paused, then said, "Oh, no. My billfold...it must've fallen out when I—" She sighed. "My cell phone's not here, either." Her gaze shot up to the mirror, then down at her lap. "I can't pay you."

"Don't worry about it. I should probably pay *you* for the entertainment."

She gathered her purse, grabbed the briefcase. "Thanks, again." The door opened. She climbed out, shut it.

Joe watched her hurry toward the brightly lit coffee shop, push through the door and go inside. He wondered how she thought she was going to get home without any money to pay another cab. Or how she planned to buy a cup of coffee, for that matter. Maybe she thought she would call her father and dollar bills would magically appear in her pocket like they had all her life.

Seconds later, the door to the coffee shop opened again and Miss Macy ran out waving at him, still clutching the briefcase with her other arm like she was afraid Harry Landau might jump out and grab it. Joe lowered his window and she bent down and thrust something at him.

"Oh, good. I caught you. I found this in my pocket." She held two dollar bills.

Joe almost blurted a laugh. Maybe her daddy *was* magic; the man didn't even require a phone call.

"Or I guess I should say my boss's pocket. *Ex* boss," she corrected. "This is his coat."

"How nice of Santa to leave you a present."

She surprised him with a laugh. "I know it doesn't cover the fare but at least it's something."

He waved the bills away. "Buy yourself a cup of coffee. Or half a cup. These days I'm not sure a couple of bucks will buy you a full one."

She gave him a look that was a little guilty, a little smug. "I found five dollars in the coat. I kept three for myself."

He took the bills.

"Well…" She offered a half-assed smile, more out of manners than gratitude, Joe decided. Then, without another word, she turned and ran back inside.

Joe prepared himself for a wait. He hated to turn off the car and the heat along with it, but he couldn't afford to waste gas. He twisted the key and the hot air coming from the vents ceased to blow. He yawned. Shivered. Studied the plate glass window across the coffee shop's front. The place looked bright and warm and inviting. Miss Macy came into view. She placed a mug on a table and sat down. What the hell. He might as well join her. Since it was long past ten o'clock, he wouldn't need to feed the meter.

When he pushed through the door, she looked up and annoyance flickered in her eyes. She cradled the steaming mug between her hands, the briefcase and her purse lay in her lap.

Joe nodded at her before heading to the counter. They were the only customers in the place. He ordered a cup, black, then gave the kid working the register the two bucks Annie had paid him.

Seconds later, Joe carried his mug to a table across the small room from his client's daughter and sat facing her. Blowing on his coffee, he breathed in the aroma, feigned interest in the television mounted at one corner of the ceiling where Jessica Simpson jerked and swayed. All the while, he felt Miss Macy watching him, and whenever he looked, her gaze skittered away. Joe stared at her a full minute just to ruffle her feathers.

She squirmed, then said, "Are you following me?"

"Nope. Just taking a break." He smiled.

She bumped her mug and coffee sloshed over the rim. Pulling a napkin from the metal holder on the table, she sopped up the spill. "Leave me alone or I'll call the police."

"I thought you were avoiding the cops?"

"I didn't say that," she snapped.

Okay, Joe decided. He'd toyed with her enough. He even managed to feel a little guilty. She wasn't the one who'd signed him up for this gig. She didn't want to be watched any more than he wanted to watch her. "Look," he said. "Believe it or not, I'm a nice guy. I happen to know you don't have any money for a cab. No phone. And it's the middle of the night." He nodded toward the door. "Come on. I'll give you a ride home for free. Or wherever you want to go."

She seemed to weigh her options, though he couldn't imagine what they were since as far as he could see she didn't have any. Finally she said, "Thanks, but I live close by. I think I'll walk."

That was a lie; she lived miles away from here. "Your choice," Joe said. *Case closed. I'm done. This was a waste of time.* He stood and crossed to the door, pausing for one last look at her over his shoulder before he exited into the falling snow. He'd call her old man now and break the deal. He was starting to feel like a stalker, he was beat, his head and knee throbbed, and pissing her off had lost all amusement. Besides, she wasn't willing to talk; he'd been a fool to think he might get some information on Reno.

Climbing behind the wheel of the cab, Joe started the engine and turned on the headlights. He fished his phone from his pocket, his focus on the coffee shop door. Before he could punch in Mr. M's number, Annie stepped out onto the sidewalk. She pretended not to see him as she turned and started down the sidewalk.

"Damn it," Joe muttered, and scrubbed a hand across his face. It was dark as pitch out, snot-freezing cold. The neighborhood was one even *he* wouldn't feel safe striking out across on foot at night. The woman was stubborn and willful and just plain out of her mind. He cursed again as he pressed down on the horn, assuring himself he was only giving her one last chance because he needed the money. Then he rolled down the window, and when she paused and turned, stuck out his hand to wave her over.

CHAPTER 4

Annie squinted into the glow of the cab's headlights. The snow was mixed with sleet now. It blew into her face, pricking her cheeks like a million tiny needles. Her toes were numb and her hair was getting damp.

But she wasn't trembling because of the cold. She didn't know what to do, where to go, or how to safely get there. Harry had her address; her apartment was the first place he'd look. She had no money for a hotel, no credit cards. And as much as she dreaded walking anywhere in this neighborhood after midnight, she wasn't sure that the cab—or the man in it—would be any safer.

Annie blinked. She knew the rude, exasperating cabbie could see her plain as day, while the lights in her face kept her from seeing him at all. She imagined the cocky expression on his face. Who did he think he was? Since picking her up outside of Landau's, he'd treated her as if he didn't have any patience for her, like she was a silly, despicable little girl he wished he'd left behind.

Annie shielded her eyes from the glaring headlight beams

as images raced through her mind. Tearing out of Landau's... the cab appearing out of nowhere like a galloping white stallion just before Harry caught up to her...the driver yelling for her to "get in" like a gallant rescuing knight from an action B movie, ready to sweep her to safety.

Convenient. Too convenient, maybe?

The knight had shed the gallant attitude by the first stoplight. Since then, he had only acted annoyed. Annie darted a glance at his vehicle's bent bumper. Some white stallion. Why was the cabbie so eager to know her business? So willing to watch after her when he didn't seem to like her very much?

And then it came to her. Just like that. A possibility that chilled her more than the snow. *Could the guy work for Harry and Reno?*

Heart thundering, she turned her back on the cab and started walking again.

A thin bent man approached from down the sidewalk, shoulders slouched and head down to ward off the blowing sleet. He wore a lightweight jacket, a bandanna tied around his head and pulled down past his eyebrows. He carried a small brown paper sack. Annie sympathized with the old guy for half a second. Then the headlights illuminated his face, and she saw that he wasn't an old guy, at all. He was a young *dude.* A young dude who slowed his pace and eyed her up and down. A young dude who smelled like rotting veggies and regurgitated whiskey and had a dagger tattooed on his cheek.

"Nice coat," he grunted.

"Thanks," Annie mumbled and stepped closer to the curb. The cab's horn blasted a second time.

She shot a quick look over her shoulder. The vehicle inched along behind her. Confused and frantic, she returned her attention to dagger-cheek.

His upper lip curled back, and maybe her imagination was only playing tricks on her, but she would've sworn the guy only had two upper teeth. They looked like fangs. "You share your coat with me, I'll share my hooch with you," he said, then jerking his head toward a nearby alley, he drew a bottle from the sack.

Oh, gawd. Her heart tripped. She turned to escape inside the diner and the lights went off inside. A Closed sign hung on the door.

Annie didn't wait for a third horn blare. She swung around and darted for the cab. She'd take her chance with the irritating cab driver. He made her uneasy, too, but at least he smelled better than the tattooed vampire. Jostling the briefcase and her purse, she opened the front passenger door, climbed in and slammed it.

The cab driver slanted a bland look her direction as he pulled away from the curb. "What? You don't like Mad Dog 20/20?"

"Hey," Annie said, panting, "I'm not in the mood, do you mind? And before you accuse me of being rude again, I'd like to thank you for waiting for me."

"I never said you were rude. *You* did."

"I said you were *thinking* it."

"I wasn't. Ungrateful, yes. Foolish and impetuous and—"

"Okay. I get it." Her heart pounded harder when she looked across at him, harder still when she thought of all the risks she had taken tonight, starting with breaking into Harry's office, all the way up to climbing back in this cab thirty seconds ago with a man who might be one of her ex-boss's goons.

Annie studied his profile a moment. She hadn't really seen his face up close until now, but the low, smooth rumble of his voice had shot a tingle straight through her the first time he spoke. Or maybe she'd overdosed on adrenaline while escaping Harry, and that had been the true source of the tingle.

She tried to be quick and discreet in her examination. He didn't look like any cab driver she'd ever seen. His features were as attractive as his voice, though not as smooth. Not even close. She guessed him to be around her age, though the years had left lines and crevices on his skin that she had been spared—which was good, as she doubted they would look as appealing on her. There was a rawness about the sharp-edged angles that made up his face. A thin white scar slashed his left eyebrow. His chin and jawline were strong and both in need of a shave. Thick dark hair curled around the edge of his coat collar.

She shifted to the steering wheel.

He flexed his fingers.

Large hands. A little rough.

And then he faced her and she saw his eyes. Dark and direct and penetrating. She swore they looked straight through her, as if he knew just what she was thinking, just what she had done.

Blinking, she lowered her gaze to his lips. Their fullness surprised her; they were the only thing soft about him. And they looked warm while she was freezing all over.

A flush of heat spread over her face. The man didn't look like a goon. He looked like every woman's rough-and-tumble fantasy.

He lifted a brow, a smug smile tugging at his mouth.

She looked away, embarrassed he'd caught her summing him up.

Wiggling her toes, she stared out the front window. She wasn't accustomed to New York winters and even wool socks didn't keep her feet warm. But she had a feeling her toes would burn holes in the soles of her Gucci boots if this guy so much as glanced at them. She couldn't wait to get home and put an end to this crazy night. The small stash of emergency cash she kept in her underwear drawer wasn't much, but it would pay for her ride with enough left over for a modest hotel room. She couldn't stay at her apartment and risk Harry showing up.

Annie suddenly realized she didn't have any idea where they were. Nothing outside the cab windows looked familiar. She tensed. Was he headed out of the city? It occurred to her that she didn't have a clue what goons looked like. Maybe they all had toe-melting stares and lips that made a woman want to pass out cold just for the chance of mouth-to-mouth resuscitation. "Where are you taking me?"

"Who knows? I haven't been given my orders yet."

"Your orders?" Her heart jumped up to strangle her.

"Yeah. From you. Where to?"

When her heart let go of her throat and slid slowly back to where it belonged, Annie told him her address. "You know where that is?"

"Yes, ma'am," he said, then chuckled.

"Is something funny?"

"I was thinking about your boss.... Judging by the way he was guarding a certain part of his anatomy, I have a feeling he'll be singing soprano for a while. You do that to him?"

"Yes, as a matter of fact." His laughter melted away another slice of her tension, and she told herself he couldn't possibly be Harry's or Reno's employee. But then, she'd proven repeatedly that she wasn't the best judge of character when it came to the opposite sex. "I hope you're right about the soprano," she said. "It would serve him right."

She also hoped what she found in Harry's briefcase would justify her taking it. Maybe she'd acted rashly, but she refused to entertain regrets. What she'd witnessed in the past few weeks regarding Harry's business dealings had convinced her more than ever that getting mixed up with Reno twenty-four years ago had ended her mother's life.

Though everything she'd recently learned about her mom seemed to indicate Lydia Macy was not the completely selfless, devoted wife and mother that Annie, with the aid of her father, had built her up to be, she could not accept that her mother hadn't loved them with all her heart. There had to be an explanation for her mother's behavior that last year of her life, one that would make sense and exonerate her. Some demon, real or imagined, must have preyed on her weaknesses, confused her, pushed her to choose the company of scum over her own husband and daughter.

As far as Annie was concerned, that demon was Frank Reno.

As her aunt Tess had guessed, Annie had come to New York to try and better understand her mom, hoping by doing so she'd better understand herself. But now she wanted more; she wanted both Reno and Harry to pay. She wanted revenge for the people they manipulated. Justice for her mother. For Lacy. For her father and herself and all they'd lost twenty-four years ago.

Leaning back against the seat, she skimmed her palm across the briefcase in her lap. If she found the evidence she expected inside it, tomorrow would be a very interesting day. If she didn't…

Annie released an unsteady breath as she contemplated what Harry might do if she found nothing…and he found her.

THE SNOW FELL FASTER. Fat, wet flakes hit the windshield. Joe switched the wipers to warp speed.

His opinion of his passenger had shifted some after watching her outside the diner trying to decide whether or not to accept his offer of a ride. If that bum hadn't showed up, he thought she actually would've struck out walking rather than climbing back in his cab. She didn't trust him.

Joe had to respect that. One thing his years on the force had taught him was that few people *should* be trusted completely. A sad way of thinking, maybe, but if he'd come to it sooner, he'd probably be a lot better off right now. Miss Macy had guts. And she might actually have a brain in that pretty head, too. He wondered if she had used it wisely with Landau tonight? Whatever she'd pulled on him must've been a doozy for her to be so on edge. If it wasn't just some irritating but harmless stunt on her part, she really might be in some serious shit.

"Here we are." He pulled to a stop alongside her apartment building.

"I'll be back in a minute with the money I owe you." She gathered her things and reached for the door, then hesitated and cast a glance out the back windshield.

Sensing her apprehension, Joe said, "Why don't I walk you up and save you the trip back down here?" When he realized she was going to protest he added, "Besides, this little escapade of yours spooked me." He feigned a shudder as he said with mock terror, "I don't want to stay out here alone."

Her smile surprised him. So did the fact that he liked it

so much. Unlike her newspaper smile, this one touched her eyes. It also revived those torrid fantasies he couldn't afford to entertain as long as he worked for her father. Fantasies that took place while spending the night inside her apartment with her, rather than outside in the hallway alone. Which is what Milford Macy would expect of him after what went down tonight.

"Come on up," she said. "I wouldn't want you to sit down here trembling with fear." She slipped the long strap of her purse over her head, across one shoulder and beneath her arm, then climbed out of the cab holding tight to the briefcase.

Joe met her at the curb and walked beside her across the snow-covered walk to the building's entrance. While she pulled out her key, he shoved his hands into his coat pockets and stood far enough back so as not to increase her anxiety. She was still unsure of him, he could see that. The image of Harry Landau holding his crotch came to mind again and Joe wondered if *he* shouldn't be wary of *her*.

The keys slipped from her fingers and landed on the cement with a jingle. When she stooped and picked them up, Joe saw that her hands shook. As she tried the lock again, he stepped up behind her. "Here. Let me." He placed his hand over hers, and she turned her head slightly and looked up, her face so near to his the warmth of her breath brushed his cheek. Her blue eyes were clouded with uncertainty as he guided her hand to the lock and, together, they inserted the key.

The door opened and Joe stepped back. He shook snow off

his hair, brushed it off his shoulders before following Annie into a brightly lit hallway and up two short flights of stairs.

At her door, she said, "I'll just be a second. Wait here." Then her eyes widened and she quickly covered her mouth and let loose a sneeze that would have easily rattled the windows if there had been any in the hallway. She lowered her hand and winced. "Excuse me. It's this perfume. I'm allergic."

"Too bad. I like it."

Joe watched her self-deprecating expression shift again to one of wariness, watched her eyes darken with the same unwanted awareness he felt in himself. He imagined lifting a hand, tracing the curve of her jaw, her smooth pale neck, the hollow beneath her throat. He pictured himself lifting the purse strap over her head, easing the coat from her shoulders as he backed her against the closed door. And as the moment stretched and energy crackled in the air between them, it was easy to pretend she wouldn't resist, that she would welcome his hands on her body, his mouth on her breast, soothing that angry red scratch.

Joe blinked and the fantasy vanished.

Annie glanced down, pink staining her cheeks. She opened the door and went inside, closed it behind her.

That's it, Joe thought, cursing quietly and raking a hand through his hair. Time to call old man Macy and put an end to all this. He would deliver his report about what had happened tonight and be through with it. Macy could take it from here. Why should Joe give a damn if Annabelle

Macy was in over her head? He didn't know her. He didn't care about her. She might look good, but she damn sure wasn't his type. He didn't even like the woman.

He started down the hallway, cursed again, returned to her door. As much as he wanted to, he couldn't walk away. And not only because he was low on cash, short on work and the rent would soon be due. Until he was certain that the woman was not in any danger from Harry Landau or Frank Reno or anyone else, he couldn't leave her alone. He'd just have to lock up his libido. It shouldn't be all that difficult; he had no use for fancy-pants women. Especially this one.

He'd keep telling himself that.

ANNIE STOOD in the dark with her back against the door, drawing deep breaths, her eyes closed. Except for her feet, she no longer felt cold and she wasn't all that afraid anymore that Harry might jump out of the shadows. Now it was the man in her hallway who frightened her. More so, her reaction to him.

On the other side of the door, she heard him utter a particularly foul word, and thought, *I couldn't agree with you more*. Good gawd. What in the hell was she thinking letting him get so close? He was a complete stranger and she could not afford to be reckless. Right now, she couldn't trust anyone except herself.

Her eyes flew open as the parallel hit her. Is this how her mother had become tangled up with Frank Reno so long ago? Had she found herself in New York alone, desperate and confused? Searching for something? Had he reached out to her and she'd grabbed hold, needing so much to cling to someone?

Stepping away from the wall, Annie flicked the light switch. The lamp beside the sofa came on, flooding the cluttered living room with a muted glow. Maybe everyone was right and she *was* like her mother, but she would not make the same mistakes. Tempting or not, she would not fall prey to the stranger outside her door. She would pay him, thank him and send him away.

A bare Christmas tree sat in the corner, the ornaments to decorate it overflowing from boxes on the floor beneath the branches where she'd left them last week. Her bathrobe and yesterday's clothes were strung everywhere. A pair of red Jimmy Choo heels she'd bought in her past life peeked out from beneath a chair. Dishes cluttered the coffee table where she'd devoured a quick bowl of cereal at 7:00 a.m. while catching the morning news.

Sighing with fatigue, Annie walked to the sofa and set Harry's briefcase at her feet. She hated to admit it, but she sorely missed certain aspects of her prior life. Namely, her weekly maid.

But for now, at least, maids were a thing of the past. Charlene, Reece and even Sara had told her she was silly not to use her trust fund money. But silly or not, Annie wanted to try to make it on her own for once in her life. The things Aunt Tawney had said about her needing a keeper still burned her ears. It embarrassed and shamed her to be so old and only now completely supporting herself. Besides, her father had set up the trust fund, and though they talked briefly at least once a week, she was still upset with him after learning he had never intended for her to take over for him at the bank. And he had hid so much about her mother for so many years. Things Annie had deserved to know.

As for the small sum she'd inherited from her mother, she refused to dip into it, either. She had never asked herself why she had saved it for so long, but now she was glad that she had. After helping put Harry away, and with any luck his uncle Frank, too, she planned to use the money to open a business of her own. It was something else she and her mother shared in common—the desire to build something, to make it their own. The difference was that Annie would succeed where her mother had failed.

Starting for the bedroom, Annie passed the end table and ran her hand across the Waterford crystal angel Aunt Tess had given her last Christmas. She snatched her bathrobe from the floor as she passed it by, and started to pull the purse strap over her head when a prickly sensation at the nape of her neck made her pause. Nothing in the apartment looked any different than it had when she left this morning. She didn't hear any odd noises. Still, she sensed she wasn't alone. Dropping the robe, she held her breath and slowly backed toward the briefcase.

The instant her hand touched the leather handle, the

lamp went out. Shoes shuffled against carpet, and the case was grabbed from her grasp. Pale light from the windows streamed in. Annie swung around and saw a shadow the size of Sasquatch looming over her. She didn't have time to cry out before the intruder shoved her onto the sofa and darted for the door carrying the briefcase.

Panic shot into her bloodstream. Gasping, she pushed to her feet and lunged for the case, catching the man's arm instead. She dug her fingernails into what felt like a sweatshirt. He tried to sling her off and when she clung, dragged her with him toward the door.

Annie shrieked, kicking and holding onto his jacket. On pure instinct, she lowered her mouth to his wrist and bit down.

The feral sound of rage he made raised the hair on her arms. While still holding the briefcase in one hand, the burly man used his opposite arm to catch her about the waist. He lifted her up like a quarter-pound rag doll. Her feet left the floor. Annie screamed and didn't stop. The man dropped the briefcase to cover her mouth.

A crash sounded. The door flew open. In the spear of light that sliced in from the hallway, she saw the cab driver leap toward them.

She twisted, kicked, the toe of her boot connected with Harry's briefcase and sent it skidding across the room.

The driver plowed into them and they all hit the floor in a tangle of arms and legs.

Annie scrambled away from the grunting, cursing men

and let them have at each other. On hands and knees she made her way to where the case lay, grabbed it, stood and stepped toward the window, praying she could make it to the fire escape on the other side before the intruder came after her. Her chest ached and her breath spasmed as, hesitating, she glanced back to where the two men blocked the door. The cab driver was on his back and taking a pounding.

Annie winced. She couldn't leave him to fend for himself. The poor guy was in this mess because of her. And she knew Harry. The man believed in doing things in a big way, in getting it "right" the first time and making an impression. This behemoth he had hired to do his dirty work was undoubtedly a pro at his job, someone with a solid background in beating the crap out of people...or worse.

Annie blinked until her eyes better adjusted to the darkness, tightened her grip on the case handle and took a deep breath. She caught sight of her Jimmy Choo shoe sticking out from under the couch. Rushing over, she picked it up with her free hand, then turned and ran toward the scuffling men. She aimed the spiked heel and started hammering away at Sasquatch's shoulders. "Stop it! Let him go! You'll kill him."

"You little—" He reached back a flailing arm and grabbed at her.

"Ow!" the cab driver shouted. "You're hitting *me!*"

It took a moment for Annie to realize the driver was

talking to *her*. She tossed the red heel aside as both men struggled to their feet, bent over, still swinging at each other.

Annie ran to the end table and grabbed the lead crystal angel, darted back to the men, reluctantly set down the briefcase. Lifting the heavy angel, she swung it hard, hitting the intruder across the back of his head.

He rose to full height, tottered.

Using both hands, Annie heaved the angel over her head, screamed like a banshee and brought it down, hitting him again.

The man fell forward into the cabbie and the cabbie fell against the door, slamming it shut.

"Run!" he shouted. "Go!"

Dropping the angel and grabbing the briefcase again, Annie bolted toward the back window that led to the fire escape. Whimpers of panic worked their way up her throat, her breath emerged in strangled bursts, her heart hammered. The purse strap had twisted around her neck and the bag banged against her bottom with each step she took. Something crashed behind her but she didn't look back. She reached the window, fumbled with the latch.

A sharp *thump* sounded. The glass above her fingers shattered. The pungent scent of gunpowder burned her lungs. Annie cried out and ducked, feeling as if her heart had exploded along with the windowpane. She reached for the latch again, twisted, shoved the shattered window up with one arm. She climbed over the sill and onto the fire escape, sucking in great gulps of fresh cold air.

The cab driver climbed through the window and stood beside her. He looked at the ground two stories below, then met her gaze.

Annie stared into his eyes for half a heartbeat, then shifted to peer at the snowy asphalt below. She turned to him, shook her head, *no*. She didn't survive Sasquatch to die jumping from a building. But she knew he was right; they couldn't risk taking the stairs. There wasn't enough time.

Taking hold of the hand he jammed toward her and hugging the briefcase with her opposite arm, she squeezed her eyes shut, gritted her teeth and they jumped.

"*Ohmi—!*"

The fall sucked the breath from her lungs. The impact on landing slammed her teeth together. She lay on her side, dazed, with Harry's briefcase wedged between her hip and the snow-packed ground and the cab driver on top of her.

Wheezing from exertion, he pushed to his knees, grabbed her hand again and pulled her up. "Let's go."

Annie seized the briefcase from the ground and ran. Her right shoulder and hip throbbed. She tasted blood on her lip.

When they reached the cab, the driver unlocked the closest door on the front passenger side, ducked in and slid across to the wheel.

Annie dove in beside him. "I don't even know your name," she panted.

"Joe." He shoved the key into the ignition. "Joe Brady."

She slammed the door and slouched down in the seat as the cab shot away from the curb on screeching tires. "I'm Anne Macy."

"Anne, huh?" He grinned. "Well, *Anne*, congratulations. You win the award for my most interesting ride of the day."

HARRY LANDAU PUNCHED IN a number on his office phone and waited through the following six rings. Puffing his slim cigar, he stared out the window at his penthouse-floor view of the frosty city below. He had worked long and hard for his piece of that view. Worked and planned, wheeled and dealed, back-slapped and brown-nosed and cheated his way up, floor-by-floor to his own private perch above the Big Apple. No way would he lose it at the hands of some bitch on a do-gooder mission.

"What took you so damn long?" he snapped when he finally got an answer.

"It's the middle of the night. I was—"

"Never mind. We've got problems. He let her get away with the case."

The man cursed. "How? She's a woman, for pity's sake. I don't know many men he doesn't outweigh by at least a hundred pounds."

"He said she bit him and took to his back with what felt like a ball-peen hammer."

"A hammer… *Sheesh.*"

"Then she slugged him with an angel. Twice."

"An angel?"

"Some fancy ornament thing. Gave him a freakin' concussion." Harry huffed a humorless laugh and muttered, "Gettin' hit by an angel must hurt like the devil."

The man chuckled, but the sound was more nervous than amused. "Maybe you should've hired her as a bodyguard instead of a waitress."

Harry thought a minute, then said, "I'll have to call Willis."

The man at the other end of the line sighed noisily. "Can't you find someone else? Someone who isn't involved? If Willis gets caught and talks, the whole line of dominoes'll topple."

"We need him. The bitch had help. Some guy must've heard the scuffle. He came in from the hallway and she took off with him in a cab. The plates match the one she left here in." Harry recited the numbers.

"You'll have Willis do a trace, right?"

"Yeah. How long will somethin' like that take?"

"Not long."

"Good. Don't be making any trips. I'll be in touch."

Harry hung up, dreading what would happen if his uncle found out about this, determined not to let that happen. He reached across his desk for Anne Macy's billfold, then opened it. Taking another hit off his cigar, he stared at the driver's license photo inside. *Annabelle* Macy, it read. *Savannah, Georgia.* Harry fluttered his eyelashes and in a high-pitched, mocking voice drawled, "Well, I do declare."

Then he blew a smoke ring into the dark and growled, "You're in over your head, lady. And Harry's gonna make sure you drown."

CHAPTER 5

The streets had started to ice over. Traffic moved at a slower pace. A thick mist filled the air as snowflakes swirled, then settled on the ground, wrapping the city in a soft blanket of white. Holiday lights winked through the frosty haze of the wee morning hours, creating a peaceful scene worthy of a Christmas card.

Joe felt anything put peaceful. *Damn radio.* All he got was static when he tried to get through to dispatch. On top of that, his cell phone was dead.

The meandering route he'd chosen might take a while longer, but if it threw off the bruiser they'd managed to escape, he didn't mind the lost time. He kept one eye on the road, the other on the rearview mirror, hoping they weren't being followed.

Wincing, he touched the tender spot beneath his left eye. Maybe it was Anne Macy he should be trying to escape. She was the one who'd given him the shiner, not that guy who'd broken in. "That fancy shoe of yours should be registered as a deadly weapon, Anne," he muttered.

"Sorry. I was trying to help."

Anne. Hmph. The corner of Joe's mouth twitched. The newspaper said Annabelle. Her daddy called her Annie. Each name conjured a different image; he wondered which one was the right fit. "Did you use the shoe to knock the guy out, too?"

"No, a lead crystal angel."

Joe chuckled. "There's some kind of justice in that."

She sat low in the seat beside him, shivering so violently he heard her teeth chattering, both arms wrapped around that damn briefcase. He was through wondering what was inside. He wanted answers. He didn't need any more convincing that whatever she'd pulled at Landau's tonight had not been just some mischievous prank. Harry Landau was after her in a big way. The man meant business. And Landau's business dealings usually included his uncle Frank. Which, for Joe, was both good news and bad. The good being that, if he could get his hands on the briefcase, he might get something on Reno, too. The bad being that, just as he had feared when he took this job, he had wound up in the role of protector.

His stomach knotted as a memory flashed through his mind. Emma Billings curled up on her bed, trembling and bleeding, terrified to silence, refusing to tell him who had roughed her up. Joe had lived with that grim image every single day of the past year.

He turned another corner, tapped the brake gingerly to

avoid skidding sideways across the icy road. As soon as Anne Macy was safely at the police station, he'd call her father; he refused to be responsible for her safety a second longer than necessary. Then he'd get with the chief and his ex-partner, Steve O'Malley, and they would check out the contents of Landau's briefcase and see just what the woman had taken to cause so much commotion.

He glanced across at her. "Hold on. Almost there."

"Where?"

"The police station."

She sat up. "I told you I don't want to go to the police."

"Why not?" He'd had just about enough of her stubborn attitude. "You might think this is some kind of amusing little game but those bullet casings on the floor back at your apartment say otherwise. You're in some deep shit, and I've been dragged right smack in the stinkin' middle of it with you." He waited for a response. Nothing. "How about you tell me what's going on? I think I deserve that much. Who was that guy?"

"I don't know, but I'm sure Harry Landau sent him."

"What did you do to piss your boss off, anyway?" He waited a beat. "What's in that briefcase?"

Frowning and nibbling her lip, she stared straight ahead out the windshield. "I'm sorry you got messed up in this." Her face contorted as she turned and looked at his puffy eye. "I'm sorry you got hurt."

Joe stopped at an intersection and rotated his shoulders.

Now, in addition to a headache, a cramp in his neck, a throbbing knee and a swollen eye, he had a pain in his back from jumping off the fire escape, and a pain in the ass sitting beside him. A great-looking pain, maybe, but annoying as hell nonetheless. "Don't change the subject. You either tell me what's in that briefcase or I'm dragging your butt in to talk to the cops."

"Please don't. I'm not sure who I can trust in there."

Only a little while ago he'd admired her for not trusting just anybody, but the woman was going overboard now. The light turned green and Joe continued on, driving slowly on the slick pavement. "You can't trust the police? Come on. Cut the drama, Sweet Tea. It's not necessary anymore. Your little self-concocted adventure has turned into the real thing."

She glared at him. "My *name* is Anne."

"Are you sure?" He arched an eyebrow and said sarcastically, "Or is 'Anne Macy' really your cover?"

"You think this is funny?"

"Oh, yeah. Where I come from, getting beat up by three hundred pounds of solid muscle is freakin' hilarious. Wait'll I tell the guys." He reached across and thumped the case. "What've you got there?"

"If I tell you and you tell the police…" She drew her lower lip between her teeth, her brow wrinkling. "I think at least one of them might be in on this."

Caught off guard, Joe frowned and said, "Define *this*."

As if gathering courage, she sighed once, then again. "I

took some files from Harry Landau's office tonight. He keeps it locked, but during the party..." She cleared her throat. "He tried to force himself on me and I slipped the keys from his pocket." Tossing her hair back, she looked straight at him, as if daring him to make a smart-ass comment, as if she was damned pleased with herself.

The woman might've led a sheltered life like her father had told him, but she was far from naïve.

"I had planned to wait until I could tap into his computer files, too, but I haven't had any luck getting his sister to slip up with the password. Lacy also works for Harry. She's a nice woman, but she's also one pea short of a pod. She thinks she can't get by without her brother's help, and he takes advantage of that by slapping her around and making threats when he thinks no one is watching."

When she hesitated, Joe said, "Go on."

"Um, at the party...things just got out of hand so fast and when he...when he..." She turned away. "Well, I knew there was no way I was going back to work for that lowlife one more day, so I took what I could get and ran."

"Okay..." Joe gripped the steering wheel tighter. "And just what do you expect to find in those files?"

"Proof he's laundering drug money through the restaurant."

His pulse kicked up a notch. "Drug money?"

She nodded. "I'm pretty sure the figures from the daily register reports won't match his bank deposits."

He tried not to let the hopeful excitement he felt show

in his expression. "If that's true, you think it'll be that simple to catch?" Joe shook his head. "If the man's laundering money and he has half a brain, you can bet he doctored the reports to cover his tracks."

"That's why I've been keeping my own set of records. For a while now, I've been writing down the daily intake figures and any cash payouts I know about, at least on the nights I work."

If she was making this up, she was a very good actress. "Why do you think he's dealing drugs?"

"I don't *think* it, I *know* it." She scooted around in the seat to face him, her eyes burning with determination. "Now I just have to prove it."

"And you know this because…?"

"A couple of weeks back, I overheard a conversation between Harry and two men. I think they were his partners—you know, his suppliers. I was hiding in his office closet and—"

"His closet?" Joe blurted a laugh.

"One of the men told Harry he'd had some trouble putting the pound together but that Harry's customer would definitely be satisfied with what he finally came up with. Those were the words he used. Putting the pound together."

"Cocaine," Joe murmured.

"That's what I thought, too. Later that night, a man came in to Landau's to eat and he sat at one of my tables. Harry pulled me aside and told me to give him the royal treatment. Halfway through the meal, Harry joined him.

When they finished, Harry asked the guy back to his office for a private nightcap."

"Was that unusual?"

"It doesn't happen often. Two other times that I can recall since I've worked there. I never thought anything about it until I overheard that conversation. So, as I said, I started paying closer attention and keeping my own records." She reached into her purse and pulled out a small leather book.

"Why is it so important to you to catch Harry Landau?"

She nibbled her lip again, glanced away from him, then back. "He's a drug dealer. *Filth.*"

The painful emotions that flickered in her eyes stirred more curiosity in Joe. He recalled what Ed Simms had said about her mother driving Frank Reno's car into the river with Reno sitting beside her. Anne Macy would've been a kid when her mother died. He had a feeling she'd done her homework and discovered the family and business connections between Landau and Reno. Undoubtedly she knew Reno was a co-owner of the restaurant. Was she out to avenge her mother? Is that what this was all about?

"I told Lacy I'd seen how Harry treated her, that I'd heard him threaten her if she didn't keep quiet," Annie continued. "I told her I'd help her. She broke down, but she was too afraid of him to tell me anything except that he was really mad at her about something. I knew she was supposed to meet him in his office before her shift started. Which is how I ended up in his closet."

"I'm not sure I understand the connection."

Shivering, Annie huddled deeper into Harry Landau's coat. "I didn't want Lacy to have to face his temper alone, so I came up with a reason I needed to talk to him and went ahead of her. He wasn't there, so I waited. I heard someone coming and peeked into the hall. Harry, Lacy and two men were headed my way. So I panicked and got in the closet."

Joe stared out at the snowy road. Old man Milford was right. She *was* impulsive. Reckless, too. If Harry was anything like his uncle, he wouldn't think twice about shooting her for spying on him. "So you heard what you heard and decided to take matters into your own hands and play detective instead of going to the cops with it. And now if the evidence you think is in that case *isn't*, you might be the one who ends up doing jail time instead of your boss. Did you think about that before you broke into his office?"

"No, because I'm positive the evidence is here. I just have to figure it out."

He decided not to inform her that even if she did find dirt on Landau, she might still be in trouble with the law for breaking into his office and stealing his files. In fact, he wouldn't doubt it if Landau's attorney found a way to use what she did to have charges dropped against his client. Snakes had a sneaky way of slithering out of tight spots. But Joe would save that piece of information for a time when Anne Macy wasn't already shaking.

He spotted the police station ahead. "You still haven't told me why you suspect the cops are involved."

She blinked at him. "Those men in Harry's office?"

Joe nodded.

"They were police officers."

His pulse rate accelerated. "How do you know?"

"Lacy said so."

"Were they in uniform?"

"No. And because the closet door was closed and I barely got a look at them in the hallway, I can't give you a good description of either one of their faces. I know their voices, though. Especially the one who talked the most. I feel sure I'd recognize his voice anywhere."

When they reached the police station, Joe passed it by. Could this be the break he'd been waiting for? It seemed too much to hope for that the missing pieces to his puzzle were in that briefcase. It was a long shot, he knew, but suddenly he felt like kissing Ed Simms for hooking him up with Milford Macy, despite Macy's very sexy, very exasperating daughter.

And he couldn't dismiss her suspicions as foolishness. Someone *had* been waiting at her apartment to ambush her. And Landau and Reno were not men a person should give the benefit of the doubt.

"I guess Lacy didn't tell you their names?" he asked.

"No. I don't think she knew. But I'm pretty sure I've seen one of them since then in the restaurant. Lacy slipped up and mentioned to me that he was a cop, then she got upset and begged me not to tell Harry. The man's voice…I thought it sounded familiar, like one of the guys who was in his office that night."

Joe's heart thumped unsteadily. "What did he look like?"

"White. Early thirties, I'd guess. Dark-brown hair. He was under six feet tall, but solid as a brick wall."

"You just described more than half the guys on the NYPD."

She frowned. "You sound as if you know that firsthand."

"I do." Joe pulled to a stop in front of a hotel. "I used to be one of them."

"You were a cop?"

"Yes, ma'am. Seventeen years. I turned my badge in last December."

Annie's stomach turned over when a possibility she'd dismissed earlier returned like a bad case of the flu. Once again, she thought of him parked outside Landau's at just the right moment, as if he'd been waiting for her. Was Joe Brady playing games with her? Could this man she was telling about crooked cops be one of them?

Pulling Harry's coat more tightly around her, she assured herself paranoia was messing with her mind. Joe Brady was a cab driver now, not a police officer, crooked or otherwise. Cabs always parked along New York City streets at all hours of the night. Nothing unusual about that. And Harry had not had time to stop and call him in the moments between when she'd run from the building until she climbed into the cab. Her ex-boss had been right on her heels the entire time.

As they pulled to a stop in front of a hotel, she said, "I can't stay here."

"Why not? You sure can't go home."

"I didn't have a chance to get any money from my apartment before Harry's friend showed up."

"Is there someone you can trust who'd let you stay the night?"

"I haven't made many friends since I've been here. I work two jobs. There hasn't been time for socializing." And she'd had enough of parties and small talk back in Georgia to last a lifetime.

"I'd lend you some money," Joe said. "But I cut up all my credit cards a while back, and I don't have enough on me for much more than a forty-dollar-a-night room. You'd probably need a tetanus shot before you slept in a place like that." He drummed his fingers against the steering wheel. "We could make a pit stop by my place to pick up some more cash."

"I guess that's my only choice."

"Actually, I thought of a third option, and it's probably the best one yet." He hesitated a second then said, "You could stay at my apartment and save us the trip back here as well as the expense of a hotel."

Annie's heart dipped, and she guessed her hesitation showed plainly on her face because Brady shifted and said, "Look, it's not much, but I promise you won't need a tetanus shot."

"That's nice of you, Mr. Brady, but I'm not in the habit of spending the night with strange men."

His mouth curved up at the corner. He jerked his head once. Twice. Three times. "So you noticed the twitch."

Heat climbed up her neck. "You know what I meant."

"What? You prefer to sleep on the sidewalk? Or take a chance on one of Landau's thugs finding you alone in a cheap hotel room?" He watched her so closely she wanted to squirm. "I'm harmless, Anne. I can't promise the same about most of the characters you might meet on the streets."

"I—"

"And call me Joe. We just dodged bullets and jumped off a fire escape together. In my book, that qualifies as bonding and the right to be on a first-name basis."

Annie laughed. And relaxed a little. If this man had wanted to harm her, compromise her, or deliver her to Harry, he'd had plenty of chances. And he could've easily left her to her own defenses more than once tonight. Instead, he risked his life to help her. "If I stay with you, I'll want to pay you for your trouble."

"It's no trouble. Beautiful women spend the night at my place all the time. Free of charge."

He was teasing her. But realizing that fact didn't stop renewed wariness of a different sort from spewing through her like tonight's Christmas party champagne. Had every ounce of rationality she possessed trickled through her body and out her big toe when Harry Landau made that pass at her? She had done some pretty risky things since her ex-boss backed her into a corner and proceeded to try to take liberties. But preparing to spend the night in a strange man's apartment might be her stupidest stunt of all. And not only because he could be an axe murderer, for all she knew. Every time Joe Brady leveled that direct stare of his on her, she caught herself wishing he'd show her his handcuffs.

But who else could she turn to? She had to trust *someone*. And, really, he hadn't given her any reason *not* to trust him.

Except for that look....

He grinned. "You can relax. I'm kidding."

"Oh." Annie lifted a brow. "So you *charge* all the beautiful women?"

Joe chuckled. "There aren't any beautiful women." A frown flickered across his face, a glimmer of embarrassment. "I mean...there are some, just not all the—oh, hell. Forget it." This time his laugh held a self-deprecating ring. "The thing is, I might be able to help you wade through those files and piece all this together. Like I said, I was a cop. A detective. I have some experience with this sort of thing. And you'll be safe at my apartment."

Annie thought she might be well-hidden from Harry at Joe Brady's place, but she wasn't so sure she'd be "safe." She wondered if she'd get a wink of sleep, knowing he was under the same roof. But his eyes were more than dark and unsettling. They looked honest, too. Even friendly. And right now she needed a friend. She decided to trust her instincts and take a chance on him.

"Okay, I'll stay with you. And I'll take you up on your offer to help me wade through Harry's files."

"Deal," he said, and pulled away from the hotel.

CHAPTER 6

"This is it." Joe unlocked his apartment door. "In the morning I'll call my ex-partner and we'll put our heads together about what guys on the force might have a connection to Landau. You could do worse than having Steve O'Malley in your corner."

He pushed open the door and Annie heard the drone of a television. For the first time, she wondered if the man had a wife, a family.

Joe motioned for her to enter the apartment ahead of him. "Ammonia," he said with a sniff. "Ma's been here."

"Hey, pal. How's it hangin'?!" a loud voice screeched.

With a shriek, Annie turned and ran face-first into Joe Brady's chest.

He grasped her shoulders, looked down at her. "It's okay. It's only Mac. I should've warned you."

"Mac?" Annie met Joe's gaze and realized they stood so close a lettuce leaf wouldn't fit between them. He felt warm and strong and safe. In that instant, she would've liked nothing better than to lean into him. Another irrational, impulsive thought, she told herself and stepped back, hearing Aunt Tawney's voice in her mind. *She is like her mother. So much so it's scary sometimes.*

Still holding her shoulders, Joe turned her around toward a far corner of the living room. "See?"

Next to the flickering TV, a five-foot-tall wire cage dominated the space where he pointed. A bright-green parrot with a yellow head perched inside of it.

"*Joey, Joey,*" the bird squawked, "*You live like a pig.*"

"Yep," Joe said, "Ma's been here all right." He reached behind to shut the door, then stepped around Annie and crossed to the bird. "I told you not to believe the lies that woman spreads about me, Mac." He glanced over his shoulder and said, "Annie, meet Mac. Mac, this is Annie."

"*Anne,*" she said, thinking it strange that he'd call her by her nickname. "Everyone back home calls me Annie. Did I tell you that?"

"No." She thought he flinched, or maybe it was only a shrug. "You just seem more like an Annie to me."

"It's a little girl's name."

"That's not what I meant. You're no little girl."

The look in his eyes made Annie shiver, then burn from the heat of a blush. What was wrong with her? She was too old to be blushing over a man.

She set down the briefcase, hugged herself, wondered about that flinch. Had she imagined it? Maybe it had been nothing more than a shrug. Or a reaction to her tone of voice. The sharpness of it had even startled her. It was ridiculous to be so sensitive about a name. Anne...Annie... what did it matter?

"I didn't even think to ask if I'd be imposing on your family," she said.

"It's just Mac and me."

As she moved in for a closer look at the parrot, the animal cut loose a catcall whistle. "*Nice set of hoots you got there!*"

"Mac! Watch your mouth." Joe cleared his throat. "Sorry. Damn bird thinks he's a comedian. Too much television. I leave it on to keep him company while I'm out. I think that's a botched line from *Dumb And Dumber*." Joe walked over to the television and switched it off.

"You might consider leaving the TV on *Sesame Street* from now on." Annie smirked at him and walked to the couch, uncertain what to do with herself now. "So how long have you had Mac?"

"A few years. Got him from some lowlifes I busted. After they went to jail, Mac was left homeless, so I took him in." Joe removed his coat and slung it over the back of a chair as he made his way to the kitchen counter. "Make yourself at home."

While he sifted through his mail, Annie slipped her purse strap over her head and shed Harry's coat, though she wouldn't have minded leaving it on. She was still shaking; she wondered if she'd ever stop. Now that things had settled down a bit, instead of her body relaxing, her muscles quivered more than ever. She placed her purse and coat on the couch.

Joe stood beside a Formica-topped counter that divided the small kitchen from the living room. Two wooden bar stools sat beneath the overhang. Annie glanced around. The television looked fairly new—a large flat-screen, she noted and wondered if he was a sports fiend. A computer sat atop a desk in the corner opposite Mac's cage. And there were books. Lots of them. Stacked neatly beneath the coffee table, on the end tables, filling the shelves of a case along one wall. Annie walked over to the case and skimmed her hand across the spines. Jack Higgins and Clive Cussler and Stephen King. She looked at her fingertips. No dust. In fact, the entire apartment was immaculately clean. So clean she was ridiculously relieved that the light had been off in her place when Joe was there. As if he would've noticed while trading punches with Sasquatch.

Joe tossed the mail on the counter. "I've got to remember to pay that phone bill," he muttered, more to himself than to her.

Annie sat on a bar stool and smiled at him. "You mean your mother doesn't pay your bills?"

"Why would she?" He opened the refrigerator, looked in.

"When you smelled ammonia you concluded she'd been here. She cleans your apartment, right?"

With his back still to her, Joe said, "Her idea, not mine."

Annie could see inside of the refrigerator. Food filled the shelves. Healthy stuff. Milk and yogurt and orange juice, fresh veggies and fruit. "I see that she also buys your groceries."

He looked over his shoulder at her, narrowed his eyes. "How do you know that?"

"You don't look like the type to buy lemon fluff yogurt."

There it was again. That look. This time with a spark in it like the one sizzling beneath her skin.

"And just what *type* do I look like, Sweet Tea?"

The low, smooth timbre of his voice exploded the spark into a million smaller ones that cascaded through her, popping and crackling like Roman candles on the Fourth of July. "Why do you call me that?" Annie asked, startled by how breathless she sounded.

One side of his mouth curved up. "It fits."

"I thought you said 'Annie' did?"

"But everyone back home calls you that. Maybe I want a name for you all my own."

"*It's a BRAND NEW CAR!*" Mac screeched, and just like that, the Roman candle fizzled along with the spark in Joe's eyes.

"Mac loves game shows," he muttered, and ducked his head into the refrigerator again. "Well, you're right, Anne. My mother does buy my groceries from time to time. And just like I figured, there's not a single thing in here that was on the list I gave her, most importantly no six-pack." He grabbed the last two bottles of beer inside and nudged the door shut with his shoulder. "Ma's determined to wean me off the stuff."

"Do you need weaning off of it?" Annie asked, then

thought, there you go, blurting things out that are none of your business.

"No," Joe answered. If her blunt question offended him, he didn't show it. "But she started when I was sixteen after I stumbled home bleary-eyed one night long past curfew, and she hasn't let up since."

"Sounds like you have a good mother."

"The best." He crossed to the counter, twisted the caps off the bottles, then handed her one. "You do drink beer, don't you?"

She met his gaze and smiled. "Not as often as I drink sweet tea."

"I thought not." He smiled back. "But I thought you could use something a little stronger after tonight."

She took a sip, and to avoid his unsettling stare, surveyed the spotless kitchen, the folded stack of towels on the washing machine, the small red poinsettias lining the sill beneath the window. "Maybe instead of beer, you need to be weaned off your mother."

He rounded the counter and took the stool beside hers. "Hey, I'm only forty-one years old. Give me some time."

"Really, you should try it. Weaning off, I mean. It's very liberating. I'm close to your age and I'm ashamed to say I just cut the cord completely myself. With my father, though. My mother passed away when I was in high school."

"Maybe that's why he babies you." Joe shrugged. "Because he lost her and he's afraid of losing you, too."

Annie jolted. "I never said Daddy babies me."

Joe hesitated. "You said you'd just cut the cord."

She tilted her head and studied him. An ex-cop, a cab driver, *and* a psychologist? Most amazing of all was the fact that what he said was exactly the truth. Her father did over-protect her out of fear. She had known that for years, but after finding out all she had the night of her wedding, Annie's understanding had turned to bitterness. She loved her dad, but she wasn't over being angry at him yet. "How do you know it's my father who's at fault?" she asked. "Maybe I'm the one who refused to grow up."

"You seem pretty independent to me."

She huffed a laugh. "I think you're the first person who has ever said *that* to me."

The spark returned to his eyes. He propped an elbow on the counter, squinted at her. "So you're my age, eh?"

"I said *close*." Annie scowled and bit the inside of her cheek to hold back a grin.

He sat his bottle down without drinking. "You lost your mom young?"

She nodded. "I was sixteen."

"It's tough losing a parent. My dad died two years ago…a heart attack. That was bad enough, but I was grown. It must've been really hard on you, losing your mom so young."

"It was. I think it was even harder on my dad, though."

"I know what you mean." He swept an arm in front of him, indicating the clean kitchen and den. "After Pop died, that's when Ma started doing all this. I think she misses having someone to pamper, so I humor her. She knows where to draw the line, so it's not so bad. We both win. She has someone to take care of, and I don't have to deal with the laundry."

"And where does she draw the line?" Annie asked.

"For one thing, she'd never show up here unannounced. She wouldn't risk putting herself or me in an awkward position."

Annie's pulse skittered at the implication. *An awkward position.* Such as finding him with a woman. Like finding him with *her.* Mac made a squawking sound and she grabbed the edge of the counter, her nerves still jumpy.

Joe frowned. "You're still shook up, aren't you?"

"I don't know what's wrong with me."

Joe twisted his bar stool to face her, tucked a strand of hair behind her ear. "You've had a rough night. Sorry if I made it any worse."

"Worse?" She shook her head and swiveled her chair around too, so that they sat knee-to-knee. "If you hadn't come along when you did, I don't know what would've happened to me."

"I was a little hard on you, though. I just wasn't sure what to think about you."

She tilted her head. "And now you've figured me out?"

He grinned. "Are you kidding? You're a mystery to me in more ways than one."

Annie almost stopped breathing. She couldn't move. His gaze held her as firmly as if he had his arms clasped around her.

"*It's just you and me again tonight, pal,*" Mac squawked.

Joe jerked and abruptly sat back.

Annie giggled, drew her lip between her teeth, looked down at her lap, the spell broken.

"Give me a break, Mac," Joe said and scrubbed a palm over his face.

He sounded exasperated and embarrassed. Maybe even a little relieved, Annie thought. She wasn't sure how to feel about that. She should be relieved, too, yet the emotion weaving through her right now felt a whole lot more like disappointment.

Joe pushed back his bar stool and stood. "You must be beat. We'll save the talking for tomorrow. Whatever's in those files, too. You can have my bed. I'll sleep on the couch."

"Do you mind if I borrow your shower?" She felt grimy and wished she had a clean change of clothes.

"Sure. No problem." He nodded toward a short hallway leading out of the living area. "In here."

She followed him into his bedroom and he opened an adjoining door, revealing a small bathroom. Annie spared a quick glance at the bed, *his* bed, which she would be sleeping in soon, and hoped his tank held plenty of cold water.

"I'll get you some clean towels," Joe said, his gaze lingering a moment on her face. "I'll set them outside the door."

"Thanks." As he turned to leave Annie said, "Oh, I need my purse." There were moist wipes inside that she could use to remove her makeup. She started after him.

"I'll get it," Joe told her.

"Thanks."

Annie shut the bathroom door, turned and leaned against it, closed her eyes. Well, this was weird. And awkward. So why did she get a little thrill just thinking about him in the next room? A humming sensation beneath her skin when she thought of sleeping in his bed, beneath his sheets, his scent wrapped around her? Maybe because the men she was used to were nothing like him. A compliment to Joe, she decided.

She sighed and opened her eyes, pushed away from the door. The excitement of the chase earlier had gotten to her, that's all. The fact that they'd almost gone to heaven together—and not in a good way—but at the hand of a burly baboon.

Annie pulled off her skirt, tugged the torn satin blouse over her head. In the mirror, she checked out the scrape on her breast, the bruises already apparent on her shoulder and hip from her fire escape dive. She stretched her sore muscles. Her whole body ached. She would get a few hours of sleep, look through the files with Joe in the morning, and depending upon what they found, take it from there. Whether she found what she expected to or not, she would need to come up with a plan of action. But she couldn't do anything about that tonight. She was too wiped out to think straight.

A knock sounded at the door. "I'm putting the towels and your purse on the floor to the right of the door," Joe said.

"Thanks," she called, then waited a beat before reaching for the doorknob. Before she could open up, a thump sounded on the other side of the wall, a clatter, then...

Joe cursed. "I dropped your—"

Some *something* hung in the silence that followed, something ominous that weighed her down with dread. And then she remembered the present Lacy had given her at the Christmas party tonight. Remembered stuffing the box into her purse, it breaking open when she hit Harry.

Burning with embarrassment, Annie winced and opened the door a crack.

Stooped in front of the bathroom, Joe held a tiny square packet between his thumb and forefinger. Along with her keys and lipstick, a stick of gum and a few pennies, at least ten other packets just like the one he held lay scattered about his feet. He lifted his gaze to her face and his eyebrows shot up.

Without thinking, she opened the door wider. "What a mess," she said, chirping a nervous laugh. "Don't worry about it. I did the same thing earlier. There are twice as many on Harry's office floor." *Good gawd.* Why had she said that?

But when his eyes shifted upward and settled on the front of her black bikini brief panties she had the distinct impression he hadn't heard a word she'd said. His stare was as hot as a beam of Georgia sunlight in July. He lingered, blinked, trailed his gaze up her belly, stopped at her bra and blinked again.

"Don't worry about it," Annie repeated, her voice a mere squeak. "My purse latch needs fixing. I'll pick those all up." If her body temperature rose any higher, she would self-combust.

He rocked a little on the balls of his feet, then stood with the packet in one hand, a towel in the other. His Adam's apple bobbed. "Here," he said, and held both items out toward her.

She took them.

The phone rang. They jumped. Joe cleared his throat then turned and left the room.

Annie dropped to her knees, scooped everything into her purse, backed into the bathroom and closed the door. She braced both hands on the sink and stared at herself in the mirror. If her heart beat any harder and louder, the police would show up all right, but not because she'd stolen Harry's files. They would arrest her for disturbing the peace.

JOE HEADED for the cordless phone on the nightstand beside his bed, wondering who in the hell would be calling at this hour.

And thinking about Annie.

Why would one woman carry around so many condoms in her purse? He laughed silently at his stupid question. *Sweet tea. Yeah, right. With a couple of shots of bourbon in it.* She had looked about as sweet and innocent as a centerfold model when she opened that bathroom door. Hair wild, cheeks flushed, nipples beaded against that black satin bra.

He reached the nightstand and lifted the phone, punched Talk. "Brady here."

"Why haven't you called?"

SMACK. Joe felt as if he'd stepped on the tracks in front of a speeding train. Nothing like lusting for a woman while talking to her father. Especially when the father was a paying client.

He couldn't get out of the bedroom fast enough.

Relieved to hear the shower come on in the bathroom, he took the phone and started into the living room.

"Where's my daughter?" The frantic tone of Milford Macy's voice had Joe hastening his step. "I've been calling her apartment half the night. Yours, too. Your cell isn't working."

"The battery died. Relax. Your daughter is with me," Joe said quietly, one eye on the closed bedroom door as he sat on the couch.

"Did something happen? God almighty as my witness, if one hair on my daughter's head is out of place you'll be sorry as a two-dollar bill. Is she—?"

"Look," Joe said, recalling with chagrin how tousled Annie's hair had looked when he'd left her moments ago. "Slow down. I'm on your side, remember? She's fine. And before you start threatening me, you might want to keep in mind that I'm doing you a favor."

"A favor? I'm paying you—"

"To follow her, not babysit, which is what I've ended up doing."

The old man's sigh traveled clearly across the line. "Is Annie okay?"

"Like I said, she's fine. But you were right to worry about Landau. He chased her out of the building right into my cab."

"He—why?"

"She stole files from his office."

A pause, then, "Lord have mercy…that girl. Thank God you were there. She probably would have gone straight to her place and Landau would've been right behind her."

Joe cleared his throat. "We did go to her apartment." He relayed all that had happened since then, stopping before he reached the part where he dropped Annie's purse and she opened his bathroom door in her underwear.

"Thank heaven she's okay." Another pause. "You haven't told her about our arrangement, have you?"

"As far as she knows, I'm only a cab driver and an ex-cop who was in the right place when she needed a quick escape."

"Good. Keep it that way. She'd never forgive me if she knew the truth. Of course, her safety is my greatest concern, but there's more than one way to lose someone, and I don't want that to happen, either."

In the space of silence that followed, Joe thought of Annie's mother and felt certain the old man did, too. Had Macy done something he regretted that had driven his wife into Frank Reno's arms?

"She thinks you're a cab driver who picked her up, yet she's spending the night at your apartment," the old man muttered in a weary, disbelieving tone. "I don't know what has gotten into her. She's always had an impulsive streak, but this goes beyond that. She's behaving just like her mother. And now she's mixed up with that son-of-a-bitch like her mother was, too."

Joe heard the ring of raw fear in the older man's voice. "She's safer trusting me right now than she would be on her own in some hotel room and she knows it. What else would you have wanted her to do?"

"Catch the first flight home, that's what."

"After midnight? I doubt seriously she could've found one."

"Well, see that she does in the morning. And I don't want her out of your sight until she's on the plane, do you understand?"

"I'll try to talk her into going home, but I can't force her to. She's a headstrong woman."

"You think I don't know that? Do whatever it takes. Hog-tie her and haul her onto the plane yourself if you have to, I don't care, just make sure she's safe."

"Mr. Macy...I might be crossing a line here, but why can't we just tell her the truth? She's an adult and I'm not much of an actor. When she realizes you were concerned enough about her safety to hire me, I bet she'll go home just to ease your mind."

Macy released a raspy chuckle. "You obviously don't know Annie. Even in light of the trouble she's in, she'd be furious with me for having her followed."

And furious at me for lying to her, Joe thought. He didn't like deceiving anyone for money. It wasn't his style. And he really didn't want to break his promise to himself and be the one responsible for her.

"I'm willing to pay you a bonus for seeing that my daughter returns to Georgia safely," Macy said, then quoted a figure.

Joe winced. The sum would easily pay for a deposit on a better place for his mother, as well as her moving expenses, with plenty left over. What the hell. Sometimes good reasons justified compromising integrity. And he could let Anne Macy in on at least some of the truth without betraying her father. If the two of them were going to get to the bottom of whatever was in those files, it might be easier if she knew certain things about his past.

"Okay," Joe said reluctantly. "I'll see that she gets safely home to you."

"What about those files?" Macy asked.

Joe heard the shower turn off in the next room. "We'll have to talk about that later. I think she's coming."

After ending the call, Joe sat back and stared at the bedroom door. For the briefest of seconds, he imagined Annie Macy stepping out of the shower naked and slick from the spray. He ordered the image out of his mind, told it to stay out. Now more than ever, she was definitely off-limits.

He glanced at the kitchen clock. 4:00 a.m. Even so, he had a feeling that the few remaining hours of the night would be long and restless.

CHAPTER 7

Annie dried off from head to toe before wrapping the towel turban-style around her wet hair. She found a tube of toothpaste in the medicine cabinet, squirted some onto her finger and made do. Finishing, she grabbed Joe's terry-cloth robe from the hook on the door, slipped it on, took her purse and exited the bathroom.

She found him in the living room sitting on the couch. When he looked up at her, she saw the same dark desire in his eyes that had been there before the phone rang. Yet there was a hint of restraint in the set of his jaw, in his body language.

She crossed to him, set her purse on the end table. "Is something wrong?"

His gaze skimmed the front of the robe before resting on her face. "No, I'm just beat. Why?"

"The phone call."

"Oh…yeah. Wrong number." He stared at her a moment. "You need anything? Another pillow? A heavier blanket?"

She shook her head. "I know I should be comatose considering all we've been through, but I'm still too wound up to sleep."

"I can't sleep, either." He gestured toward the briefcase. "Might not be a bad idea to go ahead and take a look at those files."

She took a comb from her purse. "Why are you helping me? All it's brought you is trouble." Sitting at the opposite end of the couch, a safe chaste distance from him, she pulled the towel off her head and began using the comb to slowly work the tangles from her hair.

"I'd like to say I'm just being a nice guy. And I was at first." He paused to smile at her. "But now that you've told me a few things, I also have other reasons." He steepled his hands in his lap and stared down at his fingers. "I was a narcotics officer. A year ago, I was working undercover to take down a drug ring headed up by a guy named Frank Reno."

"Oh my God," Annie whispered.

He looked up at her. "I take it you know him?"

"He's Harry's uncle. They own Landau's together."

Joe nodded.

Annie's heart rate kicked up. "Out of all the cab drivers in New York City, I climb in with you?" She realized she sounded like Mac, screwing up a movie quote, this time from *Casablanca*. She shook her head. "You're telling me that you were investigating a crime that might possibly be connected to the one I'm looking into now? And you just happen to be sitting in your cab—"

"It's not as big a coincidence as you might think. I'm still investigating Reno, just on my own time now. That's why I was sitting outside Landau's tonight. I keep an eye out for Reno and Landau whenever I can."

Suddenly it made sense to her. "That's why you stuck with me. I mean, at the diner and everything. And why you were so nosy. You knew that was Harry Landau chasing me even before I said his name."

He nodded again.

"And though you didn't know what I'd done at first, or that it might be connected to your case, you helped me because you knew he was bad news and I might be in real trouble." She tightened the robe sash, studied him. "You *are* a nice guy."

"Yeah, well…" He shifted and looked away, as if uncomfortable with her compliment. "I just wanted to make sure you got home safely and that he wasn't there waiting for you."

Making an effort to calm her breathing, Annie asked, "Why did you quit the police force?"

He leaned forward, leveling his forearms on his knees. "Things were moving along. We'd finally found what we needed to lock Reno up. A witness willing to testify against him. An insider named Emma Billings. Me, my partner O'Malley and another detective named Clayton Jones covered her twenty-four-seven. She insisted she stay at her own place, so we took the shifts ourselves. We weren't taking any chances that Reno's people might get to her to shut her up before the trial started."

The muscle along Joe's jawline twitched.

Annie laid the comb aside, dread sweeping through her.

"She had a fifteenth-floor apartment," he continued. "A nice place. Only one door in and out. I still can't figure out what happened that night. I had other things on my mind. I'd noticed a mix-up in some records earlier that day. Discrepancies in the reported amount of dope and money we'd seized on an earlier bust." He shook his head. "Maybe I was too distracted by all that. I had the midnight-to-eight shift at Miss Billings' place, and I always came on duty a few minutes early to get a cup of coffee from the kitchen and shoot the breeze with O'Malley before he left. We both talked to her before he took off, let her know the shift was changing. After he'd gone, I didn't leave the front room except once to refill my cup. There's no way someone could've got past me."

"But someone did," she whispered, seeing the truth in his eyes.

"Miss Billings was gagged and cut up a little. Terrorized. Right there in her own bed with me in the next room. Whoever did it knocked me out cold. I never saw or even heard him coming."

Annie saw a mix of anger and anguish tug at his face. "Did they fire you over it?"

"No. There was an inquiry. O'Malley and I were both checked out. Jones, too. I was suspected of everything from being drunk or drugged that night to sleeping on the job to sleeping with Miss Billings."

"Were you?"

"No." He looked at her straight on without so much as a blink. "It was all speculation. No evidence surfaced to prove any of us were negligent that night. Basically I got a slap on the wrist and a long vacation with no pay." He snagged a hand through his hair. "I couldn't go back, though. Not until I straightened everything out about that night in my mind. That still hasn't happened."

"What about Miss Billings? Did she testify?"

"She took the stand. But she changed her testimony. Said she didn't know anything. That she'd been mistaken. Reno walked, as usual, and she left the country."

"I'm sorry, Joe."

"Me, too. For Emma Billings most of all. She was in bad shape emotionally. Wouldn't surprise me if she never gets over it."

"And you don't have any idea at all how someone might've gotten to her?"

"I have part of the puzzle, just not all of it," he told her. "Earlier that evening, before my shift started, O'Malley said she had insisted on getting out of the apartment for some air. He said there was no stopping her so he took her out for an hour. We figure that's when the intruder had to have broken into her place and hid. But there were no signs of breaking and entering."

They sat silently for several minutes. Annie didn't know what to say to him. He was trusting her completely, not holding anything back. She wanted to completely trust him, too, to tell him everything about Frank Reno and her mother. Yet a little part of her held onto that piece of information. It was too personal, too painful. In the long run, she didn't see how his knowing about it could further their, now mutual, cause.

"*Lucy,*" Mac squawked, ruffling his feathers, "*you've got some 'splaining to do.*"

Huffing and shaking his head, Joe stood. "On second thought, let's save whatever's in those files. Even if we don't sleep, we should try to get some rest. No telling what we'll be faced with tomorrow."

Annie didn't argue. She saw the weariness in his face, and knew that telling his story had cost him. She watched him check the front door lock and the window latches, then followed him into the bedroom where he checked those window latches, too.

"Do you mind if I borrow a T-shirt to sleep in?" she asked.

He pulled one with NYPD in bold letters across the front from his top dresser drawer.

"I won't be far," he said as he turned to leave. "Just in the next room."

She read the thought that flashed through his eyes; he'd been in the next room when Emma Billings was terrorized, too.

"Would you mind staying in here?" she asked, hugging the T-shirt against her to stop a sudden reoccurrence of the tremors. "I'm still kind of freaked out by everything. I'd rather not be alone." She wasn't pretending. To say the events of the night had rattled her nerves would be the grossest of understatements. She needed Joe close by as much as he seemed to need to be there.

"Sure," he said. "The floor is probably more comfortable than my lumpy sofa, anyway."

AT EIGHT THE NEXT MORNING, Joe sat at the edge of the bed next to Annie. He'd already been up for a while and had showered, pulled on a pair of jeans and a shirt.

Despite the hour, the room remained dark because of the cloud cover outside. Annie lay on her stomach beneath the covers, her face toward him, her hands under the pillow. A few minutes ago, the ringing telephone had not even caused her to stir.

The apartment's old radiator didn't generate much heat. Joe thought she must be cold wearing only his T-shirt with nothing but a sheet and a blanket covering her impossibly long legs. He knew they were long because he'd opened an eye and peeked when she walked from the bathroom to the bed after changing into his shirt last night.

Joe pushed a pale strand of hair off her cheek. Why did she have to be so damn pretty? And nice. Surprisingly enough, she was that, too. Nice and funny, rash and brave, smart and sweet. He drew a deep breath. She smelled good, too. He had wanted to crawl under the couch last night when she'd called *him* nice. Yeah, he was nice all right. A nice fat liar. "Annie, wake up," Joe said.

Sighing long and deep, she rolled onto her back. "Hmmm?"

"Wake up. We need to get you out of here."

Annie frowned and opened her eyes. She pushed up onto her elbows. "What time is it?"

"Just past eight. Dino called a second ago. He's my cousin. He owns the cab. He said a couple of cops just paid him a visit. They were looking for a woman who caught a ride last night in a cab with plates that matched his."

"The one you were driving?"

"Afraid so. I figure it's you they're looking for. I guess Landau got the tag number and called it in."

Her eyes flashed distress. "They might be the cops who are working with him."

"Could be."

She scooted farther up in the bed and pulled the blanket to her chin. "You think they're coming here?"

"That'd be my guess. Dino didn't realize what's up, obviously. He gave them my name and address. If they're on the up-and-up, I doubt they'll search the place, but just in case they are in on this thing with Landau, you might want to go out the back way."

He stood and she threw off the covers, climbed from the bed and hurried into the bathroom.

While she dressed, Joe returned to the living room for her coat, purse and Landau's briefcase, then took them into the bedroom. A minute later, Annie exited the bathroom, fully dressed and carrying her boots. He gathered his makeshift pallet off the floor and threw the bedding into his closet.

Annie sat on the bed and tugged a fancy boot on over a plain wool sock. The socks surprised him. He had expected silk stockings. Or hoped for them, anyway.

"It doesn't make sense that Harry would've called the police, does it?" she asked. "Wouldn't he be jeopardizing himself considering what I think I have in this briefcase?"

"Or he's hoping you haven't had time to go through it and find anything to implicate him, so he's not worried. And then there's always the chance that you don't have what you think you do." Joe closed the closet door and looked back at her. "Look, I'll just be straight with you. As it stands right now, you might be the person in trouble with the law more than Landau. No matter what you suspect of him, the fact is you broke into his office and stole his property."

Pausing to look up at him, her boot in her hand, Annie said, "I had probable cause."

"That only comes into play if you're an officer of the law."

"Do you mean to tell me I committed a crime by taking evidence that will prove my boss is a criminal?"

"That depends on a lot of variables. For instance, did Landau routinely allow you to look at business documents? Were you given free access to his office?" When she didn't answer, he added, "The fact that Landau chased you to get them back indicates 'no'. Did anyone else see you go in there?"

"I don't think so."

"Then at least it's your word against his."

Her expression said what she didn't admit: Before rushing into her boss's office, she didn't stop to consider the consequences. She acted on impulse, driven by the need to avenge her mother, Joe guessed.

"That was nice of your cousin to call and warn me. Does he always go out of his way to help customers he doesn't even know escape the law?"

"It's me he's worried about, not you. He was afraid I might've gotten myself in some kind of bind."

"You do that often, do you?" She sent him a nervous smile.

"Only for good-lookin' women on the lam," he teased. Crossing to the dresser, he slid open the bottom drawer, took out his .38 snub-nosed, slipped it into his jeans' waistband. Then he shoved a strip clip carrying extra rounds into his pocket.

"Good gawd. You don't really think you'll need that, do you?" Annie's voice quivered.

"Just a precaution." He winked at her, hoping to ease her mind some. "Sorry there's no back door. You'll have to go out the window. I've already opened it."

She turned to the billowing curtain as if only then noticing it. "No wonder it's freezing in here." Shivering, Annie stood and slipped on Landau's long fur coat as the knock Joe had anticipated sounded at the front door.

He strode over to the open window, looked down and

scanned the alley below for signs of anyone watching his place from the back. "Looks clear but stay low and keep your eyes open until you get to my car." He turned to her and started toward the bedroom door. "At least I live on the first floor. You won't have to jump this time."

"I guess that's one consolation."

"Hang on!" he yelled toward the living room, when another louder knock sounded. He looked back at Annie and whispered, "Close the window behind you. Quietly."

"Wait a minute!" She blinked wide eyes at him. "What car are we talking about?"

"It's the Goat parked on the side street just off the alley." Reaching into his jean pocket he pulled out a set of keys and tossed them at her.

Annie caught them. "Goat?"

"GTO. You can't miss her. She's old, midnight-blue and gorgeous."

Annie looked down at the keys then up at him. "I'm scared."

"You can do this." He grinned at her, nodded, then passed through the door, closing it behind him. He walked barefoot across his living room.

The fact that he recognized one of the officers waiting on the other side of his apartment door didn't surprise him. You got to know a lot of cops after seventeen years on the force. "Hey, Willis." Joe yawned and frowned. "This better be good. You woke me from the best damn sleep I've had in weeks."

"You look like you could use it. Been a long time, Brady."

"Yeah, it has."

Randy Willis shook Joe's hand, then introduced his partner, Mike Prine. Joe sensed tension radiating from Willis. That didn't surprise him. They had worked together in the past; Willis was a part of the task force put together to take down Frank Reno. Though they had never been crossways with one another, Joe sensed from the start that Willis had no use for him. He had found out why soon enough. Joe had once targeted a fellow officer and friend of Willis's suspected of dealing. Willis and the guy had gone through the academy together.

"Strange time for a social call," Joe said, then stepped back and motioned them in.

"Wish I could say I was here for a beer," Willis said. He and Prine moved past him and into the living room.

"How's it hangin', pal?" Mac shrieked, and everyone laughed.

Then Willis turned and stared at Joe with bland eyes. "Dino Corelli says you drive a cab for him."

"Yeah, that's right. What about it?"

Prine quoted a number. "Those your plates?"

"Sounds like it."

"You pick up a woman last night sometime after midnight at the corner of 32nd and Park?"

Joe shrugged. "I pick up lots of women. Can't say I remember each and every one or where they get in."

"I think you'd remember this one." Willis handed him a snapshot.

Joe took it and pretended to study the photo of Annie. He guessed it had been shot at the Christmas party last night since she wore the same clothes she had on now.

"Yeah, I do remember her." He handed the picture back.

"You remember where you took her?" Willis asked.

"Let me think." Joe walked into the kitchen, turned on the tap at the sink, splashed his face. Turning, he recited an address close by Annie's apartment. "I'm pretty sure I dropped her off somewhere in that vicinity. She in some kind of trouble?"

"You could say that." Prine made his way over to the kitchen counter, pulled out a stool.

Joe met him there on the opposite side. Too late, he spotted the beer bottles sitting between them on the countertop.

Willis saw them, too. He came over, picked one up, met Joe's gaze and set the bottle down again. "Have company last night?"

"Matter of fact, I entertained a lady when I got off work."

Prine nodded toward the bedroom door. "She still here?"

"Nah. I avoid morning-afters whenever possible." Joe chuckled.

"She give you that shiner?"

He'd forgotten about his eye. Touching the tender spot above his left cheek, Joe winced and said sheepishly, "She was a bit of a wildcat."

Willis took another look at Annie's photograph. "Wouldn't be this little wildcat, would it?"

"Yeah, sure," Joe scoffed. "You think a class act like that would mess with me?"

Willis held his gaze. "A neighbor close by that address you just gave me said she saw a woman drive away from the apartment building in a cab around one-thirty…maybe 2:00 a.m. Said she seemed to be in a hurry."

"Must've been a different cab. That woman in the picture was my last ride of the night. I dropped her off shortly before one and headed home."

"Then you won't mind us taking a look around the place." Willis started toward the bedroom door with his partner close behind.

"What are you thinking?" Joe followed, huffing a laugh. "I got her tucked away in my bed?"

"Never know."

"I'm flattered." He held his breath as Willis opened the door. Relief sifted through him when he didn't feel a cold draft, and he exhaled when he saw that the window was shut. "Excuse the mess," he said. "If I'd known you were coming, I'd have tidied up."

RECLINED IN THE BACK SEAT of Joe's GTO, Annie huddled beneath Harry's coat with the briefcase and her purse on the floorboard beside her. She wished she and Joe had looked at the files last night. Until he had mentioned the possibility that she could've committed a crime, the thought had never crossed her mind. Now her urgency to find evidence against Harry increased tenfold, even if it didn't lead to Reno.

Joe's apartment was off-limits now, as was her own. She had recognized the voice of one of the officers at his front door—the one Joe had called Willis—as that of one of the two men who had been in Harry's office the day she hid in his closet. If the guy suspected Joe had helped her, they would be watching his place from now on.

A car engine rumbled to life somewhere nearby. Annie resisted the temptation to look. She hoped the cops were leaving. She was fast turning into an icicle, and Harry's coat offered little comfort. At least a foot of snow covered the ground, and frigid wind hissed through every crevice of Joe's car.

After at least ten more minutes of waiting, Annie's teeth were chattering nonstop. She thought she might cry with relief when the front driver's door opened and the overhead light blinked on briefly before the door closed again. Instead, she sneezed.

"Holy shit," Joe said. "If Willis and his partner didn't hear that a mile away, they're deaf."

"I couldn't help it. I probably have pneumonia from waiting out here." She started to sit up.

"Stay down," Joe snapped, without turning to look at her.

"If they're watching my place, they probably expect I'll leave in the cab, but I still don't want to take any chances."

Annie stared up at the back of his head. "Does your heater work?"

"Yeah, but I'm not starting the engine for a while yet. Like I said, they could be hiding out somewhere close by watching for me to take off. Sorry I had to leave you out here. I didn't think it would be smart to leave the apartment right after they did." He paused, then added, "Looks like this snow's not letting up."

"Where are we going now?"

"I'm not sure."

Still shivering uncontrollably, Annie listened to the tap, tap, tap of Joe's fingers against the steering wheel. "That man you called Willis? He's one of the policemen I heard talking to Harry when I was hiding in his closet. I recognized his voice."

The tapping ceased. "You're sure?"

"Positive."

"We need a safe place to stay until we can get you on a plane out of here. Any ideas?"

"A plane?" Annie lifted her head from the seat. "Where am I going?"

"Home."

"You mean Savannah?"

"If Savannah's home."

"I'm not going home."

"Why not? You'll be safe there with your family."

"But if Harry finds out where I am and follows me there, then I'll put my family in danger, too."

A horrible thought struck her. What if Harry talked to Reno about this? About her? Would he remember the name Macy? Or had he completely erased her mother's death from his memory? At that moment, she prayed that he had. The thought that he might remember, that he might threaten her family in order to get to her, made Annie sick with apprehension.

"Joe, there's something I haven't told you." She sat up.

"Annie, I told you to stay down!"

She slumped in the seat again. As she explained her mother's connection to Frank Reno, she expected him to express surprise. Or in light of his own ongoing investigation of the man, irritation that she hadn't shared this bit of her family history last night. But Joe listened without comment.

When she finished, he released a long breath. "This is your father's problem, too. From way back. He should be in on this. Let him help you. Help each other."

"I know I have to tell him. I have to warn him. And I will. I'll call him."

"My phone is dead. I didn't think to charge it when we got in last night."

"Then we'll find another one. But I don't want to go to Georgia." She remembered Aunt Tawney telling Tess that she couldn't be counted on to follow through with anything. "I'm not turning this over to you and running away, Joe. I started it and I'm going to finish it."

"I'm not asking you to turn it over to me. We can stay in touch. You don't have to be here to—"

"I'm forty years old and I only found out recently the details surrounding my mother's death. My father hid it from me. He built her up in my mind as this humming little June Cleaver wife and mother and I bought into it even though I think I knew deep down it wasn't true…that she was unhappy. I've spent twenty-four years trying to live up to that image of her he created. To stay close to him and make up for what he lost by doing what I thought were all the right things that would make him proud." She thought of the long hours she'd put in at the bank. "Turns out, what I was doing wasn't what he wanted at all. So now I'm doing what *I* want to do. Sometimes I think he's been afraid all these years I'd follow in her footsteps if I knew the truth."

After a long pause, Joe said, "Maybe he was right to worry about that."

"Don't you start with me, too. I am not *just like my mother*, damn it."

Her own words startled her. Until now, she had not admitted to herself how much it bothered her for people to make that comparison. Before, she'd always thought they meant she was a nice, well-bred lady who did what was best for her family, who made them proud. Now she knew oth-

JENNIFER ARCHER   127

erwise. They meant she was never satisfied, impetuous, flighty. Annie wasn't sure which image bothered her more.

"I didn't get mixed up with Harry or Reno out of desperation or naïveté," she told Joe. "I sought them out with a purpose in mind, knowing exactly what kind of men I might be dealing with."

"You don't think your mother knew that, too?"

Annie didn't want to believe it. If her mother *had* known, that meant she'd willingly tried to go into business with a crook. "No," Annie insisted. "I don't. I think she needed help, she wanted out of her life with my father, and Reno came off as a friend to take advantage of that."

She told Joe about her conversation with Karla Wilshire, the woman who'd last seen her mother alive, about Reno taking Lydia's money, their fight on the night of her death.

"This isn't the way to prove something to your dad, Annie."

"I'm not trying to—"

"It's not a way to prove something to yourself, either. You may be angry with your father—"

"I never said that."

"You don't have to. It's obvious, and if I'd been kept in the dark all my life about something I deserved to know, I'd be angry, too. But, here's the deal. I'm not sure where to take you, and I'm not even sure the airport's an option. Willis didn't buy one word I said. If I were him, I'd be checking the airports for you." Joe exhaled noisily. "He'll probably be paying my mother a visit and questioning Dino again, so we can't go to either of them. In fact, I'm going to tell my mom to stay with a friend of the family for a while."

"I'm so sorry I got you involved in this. Now your family…" Annie closed her eyes. "I'll understand if you don't want to help me anymore. All I ask is that you don't go to the police for a while. At least give me some time to look through the files."

"Aren't you forgetting that I was involved in this long before I ever met you?"

She hadn't forgotten. And the irony of that still didn't escape her, either.

"I'm not going to leave you on your own, Annie. Especially not now, not that I ever would have." Joe turned on the engine and slowly eased away from the curb. "Randy Willis was part of that task force I told you about, the one I was working with to catch Reno."

"You're kidding?" Annie shuddered as warm air blowing from the vents up front found its way back to her.

"He didn't like me because I'd worked undercover to target some dirty cops."

"If Willis was honest, why would that bother him?"

"He wasn't the only one on the force it bothered. Some cops believe you stand up for each other, cover for each other, no matter what. They have it out for any officer who goes against that."

"Do you think Willis's association with Harry might be involved with what happened to Emma Billings?"

"It might be a long shot but, yeah, that's crossed my mind."

As they moved along the road, Annie watched the city lights pass through the window. After a long stretch of silence, she said, "You think I could sit up now?"

"Sure. Go ahead."

"Thank you. I feel like a fugitive."

"Maybe that's because you are," he said dryly.

Her laugh sounded jittery. "Wait'll I tell my friend Sara. She'll never believe it."

"Don't make light of this, Annie. The repercussions you might face for stealing those files are no small thing. Neither is the fact that I'm aiding and abetting a fugitive."

Annie felt a slow sinking sensation in her chest. "I prefer the word 'borrowed', if you don't mind. I *borrowed* Harry's files. I'll gladly give them back after I have the information I need. Anyway, I'd rather not think about possible repercussions."

"We have to think about them. Look, if we do find something on Landau, it might at least put you in a better position. What we need is some place out of the way where we can hole up until we work all this out."

"My aunt Tess has a house in the Catskills. It belonged to one of her old boyfriends. He left it to her in his will."

"He died?"

"He was a really *old* old boyfriend. Especially considering that my aunt was only about thirty-five at the time."

"Hmmm." Joe met her gaze in the rearview mirror and his brows lifted.

"You'd have to know my aunt. It's not how it sounds. She really cared for him."

"They always do."

Annie scowled at him. "Anyway, I know where she hides a spare key. I think her place is about a three-and-a half or four-hour drive from here."

"In these conditions, a four-hour drive might be more like six or seven. But if we get started now, maybe we can beat the worst of the blizzard."

"The name of the town is Pinesborough."

"We'll stop along the way for a map."

The vehicle ahead of them fishtailed. "You think your car can handle it?"

"This old beauty?" Joe glanced back at her. "I'd bet money on her. Besides, I have tire chains in the trunk if it gets too bad. We'll give it a shot. I can't think of a better idea, can you?"

"No. Aunt Tess didn't have any other old boyfriends from around here as far as I know." She leaned forward, settled both forearms along the top of the front seat. "Joe?"

"Yeah?"

"Thanks."

"Don't thank me," he said tensely.

"Why not?" she asked, baffled that he'd be uncomfortable with her gratitude. "Like I said, I can't imagine what would've happened to me if you hadn't been hanging around outside Landau's. Or if you hadn't been willing to help me."

"If it makes you feel any better," he said, "meeting up with you last night might've been the best stroke of luck I've had in awhile myself."

CHAPTER 8

Morning sunlight strained through the gray, moody gloom. Joe stopped at a gas station that doubled as a convenience store and bought fuel, strong coffee and stale Danish. Then he stood in an ancient phone booth out front and dialed Dino's number, keeping an eye on his GTO. Beyond the frosty windows, Annie ate her make-do breakfast.

"Hey," Joe said when his cousin answered. Holding the phone to his ear with his shoulder, he shoved both hands into his coat pockets and shivered. "I'm in a bind. Would you call Ma for me and fill her in? Don't scare her, just say enough to make her cautious." He briefly explained the situation and clued Dino in on what to expect. More questions from police officers, the possibility of being followed. "It's too tied-in to be a fluke," he finished, thinking aloud more than confiding in his cousin. "If what Anne Macy suspects is true, Willis is making drug deals with Harry Landau."

"And with Harry being Reno's nephew…" Dino gave a low whistle. "Man, oh man. I see what you mean."

"Yeah, pretty damn cozy, isn't it? Unless my memory's

playing tricks on me, Willis was at both of those raids last year where dope and money disappeared afterward."

"So you think he was skimming?"

"It's starting to look that way. And when he heard I'd uncovered differences in the reports, he decided to shut me up before I dug deeper."

"By making it look like you were the cop with a hand in the pot, instead of him." Dino whistled again. "You think he might've had something to do with shutting up the Billings woman, too?"

"Could be." Joe pulled his hands from his pockets, rubbed them together, trying to generate warmth. "I better get back on the road. Take Ma to stay with Ed Simms and don't let her give you 'no' for an answer, okay? And fill Ed in for me. I tried him a second ago but only got his machine. I'll call him again later."

"You got it."

"And would you stop by my place and pick up Mac?"

Dino groaned. "I was sorta hopin' you'd forget about that little smart-ass. He doesn't like me."

"It'll just be for a few days, at most."

"Fine, but I'm warning you, if that sarcastic pile of feathers bad-mouths me I'm gonna open his cage and let the cat in."

Laughing, Joe told his cousin goodbye and broke the connection. Next, he called Steve O'Malley, hoping his ex-partner might be persuaded to do some digging on Willis and Prine from the inside. When he didn't get an answer, he called the station and, without revealing his identity, learned that O'Malley wouldn't be back for three days.

As Joe walked to the car, he remembered Steve mentioning that he and Kathy might have an early Christmas with her family in Boston. He hoped Kathy hadn't taken a turn for the worse. Recently, her cancer had come out of remission. Though she'd been holding her own, Joe knew that could change in the space of a day.

He knocked on Annie's window and she rolled it down. "Your turn," he said.

"How did your mom feel about going to stay with friends?"

"Didn't talk to her. I called Dino and told him to tell her."

"Chicken," Annie teased.

"If I called her, she'd ask so many questions we wouldn't get back on the road until after dark."

Annie opened the door and climbed out. As Joe followed her toward the pay phone, she glanced back at him. "You can wait in the car where it's warm. I'll be okay."

"I'll feel better out here with you." He looked over his shoulder at the road.

Annie paused halfway to the phone booth. "Are we being followed?"

He shrugged. "Can't say. Pays to be careful, though." He knew she'd be too nervous to sleep if he told her he suspected they'd been tailed since leaving the apartment. Joe thought he'd ditched whoever it was before he'd taken the exit, but he wasn't going to assume.

Turning, Annie proceeded to the pay phone, stepped inside, lifted the receiver and looked back at him. "Your car is ten steps away. I don't need a babysitter. I'm a big girl."

The stubborn tilt of her head made him smile. "Concentrating on my driving would be a damn sight easier for me if you weren't."

Her eyes narrowed. "What's that supposed to mean?"

But he could see that she was only being coy. She understood his insinuation. Grasping her free hand, Joe turned it up and dropped a few quarters onto her palm. "Just dial, Sweet Tea."

Several seconds later, Annie argued with her father while Joe shifted awkwardly beside her. No doubt Milford Macy was upset with him for not convincing Annie to fly home. But things had changed since their phone call last night. Willis and Prine had entered the picture. Besides, the old man should've known better. Annie might've been easy for her father to manipulate in the past, but finding out the truth about her mother's death had obviously spurred a rebellion in her.

"We'll be safely hidden at Aunt Tess's," Annie said into the phone. "Daddy…" She sighed. "I'm not trying to punish you. Not that you wouldn't deserve it." Another sigh. "Just keep an eye out. I doubt they'd send anyone there, but we're dealing with Harry Landau and possibly his unc—I know you can take care of yourself, and guess what? So can I." She took the receiver away from her ear, and with her lips pursed, held it in the air for several seconds so that Joe could hear Macy's agitated voice. Pressing it to her ear again, Annie said, "The man I'm with used to be a policeman. A detective. What better bodyguard could I possibly find?" Raising her gaze skyward, she handed the receiver to Joe. "He wants to talk to you."

Well, damn. How did Macy expect him to talk about anything with Annie standing beside him listening? He took the phone. Drew a breath. Held it then exhaled. "Hello, sir. This is Joe Brady."

"I thought we agreed you'd put my daughter on a plane?" the old man hissed.

"I suggested that, sir." Joe avoided Annie's stare. "It seems she isn't interested in going home. And I'm not sure it's a good idea, anyway. Those men she told you about will probably be expecting her to try to catch a flight somewhere."

Annie crossed her arms, tapped the toe of her boot against the snow-covered sidewalk.

"Our deal still stands," Macy said after a long hesitation. "Just keep her safe until I can decide what to do to help the two of you."

Joe swallowed, turned away from Annie. All he needed was for her clueless, know-it-all bigwig father to stick his nose in where it didn't belong and make things worse. "You don't need to worry about it, sir. I can handle this."

"I can't just sit back and do nothing. I'm worried sick. Keep me informed or I'm coming up there."

"No need for that."

"I still don't want her knowing anything about our arrangement. She's upset with me enough as it is. There's no reason she should ever find out. Your job is just to keep her safe and continue to tell her you're sticking with her because of your past dealings with Reno."

"I am."

"Good job making that look like a coincidence, by the way. Just leave out the part about the bonus I'm paying you." He released a noisy breath. "The check's here waiting for you, Brady. Have her home safely before Christmas and it's yours."

Joe's stomach clenched at the thought of continuing to deceive Annie. From the start, he had been wary of Milford Macy's intentions in hiring him. And now that he was getting to know Annie better, her father's deceptive method of trying to keep her out of trouble was starting to really chafe him.

But a troubling new possibility had entered Joe's mind. If Annie found out what he and her old man had been up to behind her back, she might just get angry enough to take off on her own. And Joe couldn't let that happen.

HARRY LANDAU DABBED blood off his face with a warm, damp towel as he made his way into the bedroom to answer the telephone. "Talk to me," he said into the receiver, irritated by the interruption in his routine almost as much as by the razor nick on his chin.

The caller coughed repeatedly, then said, "I had a message you'd called."

"Thought you should know that Willis paid a visit to the cab driver. You might know the guy. He's an ex-cop name of Brady."

Silence emanated from the other end of the line, then, "Damn."

"I was afraid you'd say that. Is he trouble?"

"Maybe." The caller blew his nose.

"You have a cold or something?"

"A big one." He coughed again. "How'd the woman end up in Brady's cab?"

"Like I said, he was parked right outside the building when I chased her out."

"If I know him, that was no coincidence."

Harry applied more pressure to the cut. "Whether or not he was in on this from the beginning, Willis thinks Brady's helping her now. She wasn't at his place when they dropped by, but she might've been earlier. Brady took off shortly after Willis and Prine left. Willis thought he might lead them to her but the morons lost him in traffic."

"With Brady involved, things just got a lot more complicated for everyone. Me most of all."

Harry pulled the towel away from his chin, checked in the mirror over his dresser and saw that the bleeding had stopped.

"You sure those files are worth all this trouble, Landau? Could anyone really find anything incriminating in them?"

"If they knew what to look for. Anne Macy works days at a bank. I don't know if she has the brains to put it all together, but she was suspicious enough that she took the files. That's enough to make me worry." Harry still couldn't figure out why she was so bent on getting him into trouble just because he'd tried to have a little fun with her.

The caller sighed long and deep. "This sucks. I wasn't expecting—"

"Don't worry," Harry said, "Willis will find her."

"Tell him not to hurt her. Or Brady, either. I don't want to be involved in anything else like that again, understand? He just needs to scare her enough that she'll back off."

Harry stared at the red nick on his chin and felt his mouth go dry. He doubted this guy would be as eager for leniency toward the charming Miss Macy if he knew what was really at stake. She'd carried more away in that briefcase than a few expertly doctored documents. In fact, Harry wasn't worried about those at all. The prospect that she might discover what he'd hidden in the lining of the case, though, terrified him. He had considered it to be his personal insurance policy should disaster strike.

Instead, it just might *be* the disaster.

LATE THAT AFTERNOON, sparse traffic moved slowly along the snow-packed highway. Joe tried the headlights, found that the reflection off all the white snow only made visibility worse and turned them off again.

Annie had spent the last couple of hours shuffling through Harry's files and talking nonstop in an effort to keep Joe awake. He refused to let her take a turn at the wheel. Since she had little experience driving on ice, she didn't argue.

"Everything adds up," she said. "The register reports and expense receipts, the deposits, my notes. I don't understand it."

"I'm sure Landau has a lot of experience in creative accounting."

Frustrated, she closed the briefcase and glanced out the window. "I hope they don't close the road."

"I'm surprised they haven't already. If this doesn't let up soon, we'll look for a motel."

"We'll be lucky to find a vacancy. This four-hour drive has turned into a marathon."

Despite the treacherous weather, she felt more at ease now that she and Joe were partners of sorts. Before, as far as she'd known, he had just been a stranger helping a woman in trouble. But after hearing his connection with Reno and his suspicions about Willis, she knew he, too, had a stake in nailing Harry Landau. A bigger one than she did, actually.

She set the case in the back seat. "It's funny how things happen, isn't it?"

"What do you mean?"

"Willis. Harry and Reno. Us. The way we're both tied to them in different ways. Any one of a hundred or more cabs could've been at the right place at the right time last night, but it was yours. Do you believe in karma?"

He remained focused on the road ahead. "You mean that something in the universe might've thrown us together for a reason?"

"Exactly."

"No." He shifted in the seat and kept his gaze focused on the road.

Leaning against her door, Annie studied him. When he wasn't smiling—which was often—he had a hardness about him, a cynical set to his jaw, the demeanor of someone who'd fought his way out of tough times more than once. She wondered what he would think of the world she had grown up in, her privileged background.

Watching him, she compared him to the men in her past. Annie couldn't imagine Joe wearing cuff links and doubted he owned any. She'd bet Harry's briefcase that he had never played nine holes of golf in his life, much less eighteen, and probably didn't know a birdie from a bogie. Joe would undoubtedly consider it a crime to spend a hundred dollars on a bottle of wine, and when she really thought about it, she wasn't so sure she disagreed.

She recalled the look in his eyes last night when she'd opened the bathroom door wearing only her underwear. When Joe Brady pursued a woman, Annie felt certain family finances did not influence his interest.

Her face warmed as a blush spread up her neck. Since

meeting him, she was only starting to realize just how much she had missed out on during her life. For one thing, she'd missed out on *that look*. No man had ever stared at her before with so much heat in his eyes. No boyfriend, none of her three fiancés. Annie suspected they'd all been more attracted to her father's wealth than to her. But those sparks in Joe's eyes last night had ignited because of *her*, not her father's money. They had sizzled for the woman she really was, not the woman she'd tried for years to be.

She glanced at Joe's mouth, his hands on the wheel. Rough hands, not soft and manicured. Her nerve endings hummed beneath her skin. *Oh, yeah*, she'd missed out all right. Who needed cuff links, country clubs or high-dollar wine when men like Joe Brady were out there roaming about? Why hadn't she known? She had assumed his type only existed in fiction—paperback detective novels and high-adrenaline movies. She had the craziest urge to ask him to pull over at the next motel even if the snow stopped falling, the sun came out and the roads miraculously cleared.

"Have you ever been married, Joe?"

"Once. Right after I finished at the academy. If you can call it a marriage. It lasted less than a year. We were too young, and I had a mistress."

"Oh." She sat straighter. Damn it. At the core, were all men the same?

He slanted her a look. "My job was my mistress."

"*Oh.*" She smiled.

"My wife couldn't handle that. It was probably for the best." He paused, then asked, "How about you? Ever married?"

She shook her head. "I've been engaged three times. The last time I almost went through with it. I had on the dress, the church was full of guests, the music was playing…."

"What happened?"

"I caught him giving the wedding planner a medical exam."

His brows shot up. "I take it the guy wasn't a doctor?"

"Nope, a banker. But the wedding planner isn't the real reason I backed out. I was going to, anyway."

He took a moment to study her before returning his attention to the road. "So you've ended three engagements. Why?"

Until recently, she didn't think she could've answered that question. But now she knew. *Especially after last night.* "I didn't like the way they looked at me. Or, I should say the way they *didn't* look at me. And, bottom line, deep down, I didn't want the sort of life they offered."

"Why were you with them in the first place, then?"

"I guess because they offered the sort of life I thought I was *supposed* to want."

Joe was quiet for a moment, then he said, "Any man who doesn't look at you the way I think you mean is a fool."

Annie couldn't help it; she grinned at him. "That's one of the nicest things anyone's ever said to me."

"I'm just telling it like it is." He smiled.

She tilted her head. "Did anyone ever tell you that you

can be charming when you try? And you're not so scary when you smile, either."

"I'm scary, huh?"

"Terrifying. But your smile… You should use it more often. I bet it gets you lots of girlfriends."

"I've had a few." He shrugged. "No one special."

"Never?"

"Nope. Not since my wife. And that was more drama than anything else. Like I said, we were young."

Annie pursed her lips and studied him. "So, what? You're one of those guys who have a lot of one-night stands with strange women?"

He blurted a laugh. "There've been a couple of weird ones."

She punched his shoulder. "You know what I meant."

"I'm not big on one-night stands, but—" He shrugged. "Once or twice." He frowned at her, though his eyes held a gleam of amusement. "You're as nosy as my cousin Dino."

She yawned. "I'm just curious." And to her surprise, a little bit jealous of his one or two overnight flings. She yawned again, snuggled closer to the door and closed her eyes.

"Hey," Joe said. "Wake up, Sweet Tea. If I have to confess, so do you."

Annie opened one eye. "Me?" She made a huffing sound. "I've reached the age of—" She stopped herself, opened her other eye and smirked at him. "Let's just say, I've been around for a while and I've never once had a one-night stand. Can you believe that?"

"Yes," he answered without missing a beat. The corner of his mouth twitched.

"Why is that so unsurprising to you?" Annie asked defensively.

"You just don't seem the type."

She lifted her chin and frowned. "You saw all those condoms in my purse."

"I have a feeling there's another explanation for those, though I'm having a tough time figuring out what it is."

Annie opened her mouth to tell him, then shut it, deciding she didn't want to confirm that he was correct about her. She wasn't sure why his certainty that she wasn't a loose woman made her feel like a prude. "What 'type' do I look like?"

"Where are you headed with this line of questioning?"

"Obviously you've summed me up and I'd like to know what you've concluded."

"Okay…" He hesitated. "You're college educated. And while in college, you were a nice sorority girl, most likely. A card-carrying member of I-Felt-A-Thigh or I-Ate-A-Zeta."

"Those would be fraternities, not sororities," she said smugly. She'd heard all the crude spoof names for Greek organizations before.

"Let's see…" He squinted at her. "You come from money." He winked. "The accent gives you away, along with a few other tendencies." He waited for her to say something and when she didn't, continued, "Back home in Georgia, you went to lots of fancy parties with your fancy friends, worked now and then at a friend's boutique or some other such token job just so you'd feel like a contributing member of society, did a little volunteer work on the side." He shot her another look, asked, "How am I doing?"

She stared at him blankly. "Go on."

"A lot of guys over the years have tried to get in your pants, but only the three you were engaged to succeeded. A lot of other guys wanted to try, but they didn't have the guts. They thought a girl like you was out of their league and they were right."

"So you're saying I'm a snob?"

"No. You just had your standards. Inbred since birth and you didn't even know it."

Her heart was beating too hard. She felt like he'd opened her closet and everything ugly she'd ever owned came tumbling out. Annie wasn't wild about the picture he'd painted. The portrait was of a woman she didn't want to be.

When Joe spoke again, his voice had lost some of its jest. "And even though there were plenty of times you wanted like crazy to move away or do something with yourself that might not be the sort of thing you were raised to do, you held back. And part of the reason for that was that you loved your family and didn't want to hurt or disappoint them, your dad most of all. Especially after what he went through with your mother."

Annie couldn't speak. How could this man she'd known

less than twenty-four hours see so clearly into her head and heart and soul? He seemed to know her better than anyone else, seemed to *get* her more than anyone ever had.

"That's about it," Joe said quietly. "Was I right?"

"About some parts." She kept her voice light.

"Which ones?"

"I'll let you decide." She managed a smile, though her chest felt tight.

He frowned. "You know this was all in fun, right? You asked me to do it. I—um, didn't mean any of it as an insult. Who am I to—" The car lost traction and veered toward the shoulder. Cursing, Joe set the vehicle straight again. "Excuse my language," he said.

"You're excused." She steadied her nerves, determined to recapture the teasing banter between them again. "Now, my turn to tell you about you."

He narrowed his eyes. "You didn't say that was part of the deal."

"Now you know." Annie cleared her throat. "You're from a large Italian family. Cousins by the dozens. Aunts and uncles. No brothers or sisters."

"Does the name Brady sound Italian to you?"

"Your mother is Italian, your father was Irish." She pursed her lips and studied him. "And probably a cop, too."

"That was easy enough to guess."

"You were the stereotypical bad boy growing up. A real tough guy. Cocky. Adored by your mother, swooned over by every teenaged girl in the neighborhood. And some of their mothers."

He slid a smug look her direction. "That was also easy."

"Which brings me to your huge ego," she added. "Hmmm, what else? Your mom tried to teach you manners, but only had partial success. I know that because whenever you curse, you always apologize afterward."

"I do?"

She nodded.

"Damn." Grinning, he added, "Sorry."

Annie laughed. "Your parents were hard workers. They saved every penny they could spare to send you to college. You weren't interested in college, though. You were always just one step away from getting busted for something. So you decided if you couldn't beat the law, you might as well join it. So you broke your mother's heart and became a cop like your father, dooming her to more long nights of worrying, like she had over her husband all their marriage." She paused. "Well?"

"Not bad. You were wrong about a couple of things, though. And left some things out."

"Such as?"

His jaw twitched. "Nothing you want to hear."

"But I do." She leaned closer to him. "Really."

He blew out a long breath. "I had a brother five years younger than me. He got mixed up with a gang and died of a gunshot wound when he was fourteen. My dad was never the same."

Annie's stomach dropped all the way to her toes. "Joe… I'm sorry. I didn't mean to—"

"Don't sweat it. We got through it."

Listening to the steady swish of the windshield wipers, Annie said, "I feel like the biggest idiot loudmouth on the face of the earth."

His cheek twitched. "I wouldn't say that. Not the *biggest*, anyway."

She appreciated his teasing tone, knew that he was trying to make her feel better. "Sometimes I start feeling so sorry for myself, like I'm the only one who has suffered a family tragedy or gone through problems." She faced him, blinked. "All your less-than-flattering guesses about me, about my life—"

"I was having a little fun with you."

"They were right on target."

He briefly met her gaze. "I didn't finish telling you what else I see in you."

Annie winced. "I'm afraid to ask."

"You have guts. You're one of the strongest, smartest, most fearless women I've ever met."

She swallowed, murmured, "I'm not fearless."

"Maybe not, but you don't let fear stop you."

"You don't think I'm crazy for taking those files? For trying to find evidence against Harry that might lead to Frank Reno?"

"No." He shook his head. "Seeking justice is never crazy. That's what you're doing, isn't it? Avenging your mom? Not only her, but your dad and yourself, too."

She turned to the side window. "I don't know why it's so important to me. I mean, at first I was convinced Frank Reno must've bribed her or blackmailed her. Or done *something* terrible to my mother for her to get mixed up with him. I even created this ridiculous scene in my mind where he forced her into that car and drove her into the river himself wearing a life jacket." Annie blurted a short humorless laugh. "But the more I learn about her—it stands to reason she wasn't an innocent in whatever took place."

Annie faced him. "Karla, the woman who was her friend here, she didn't say my mother and Frank Reno were having an affair. She hedged, but I could tell the truth just by her expression. Another friend of my mother's back home told me that Mom was planning to leave my dad. Probably me, too. To go into a partnership with a lowlife thug. Most likely to carry on an *affair* with him." Annie shook her head. "Even knowing all that, I still want to blame him, isn't that silly? I want to believe there was more to it, something that would clear her of everything and make sense of it all."

"That's not silly, Annie. She was your mother. And if I know Frank Reno, there *was* more to it."

"The thing is, no matter what we find in these files, I'll probably never know for sure about her." She exhaled a long breath. "My father…his heart broke when he lost her. He clung to me and he's never stopped clinging."

"That must be hard on you."

"Sometimes." She suddenly felt as cold as it looked

outside. "What if I'm wrong? What if my mom knew exactly what she was doing? Sometimes, I feel like she's the one I should hate, not Reno. She hurt my dad so much." *And me*, Annie thought. *She hurt me, too.* "She should've been at home with us, not here running around with a bunch of losers doing who knows what." Her voice broke, and Annie continued to look out the window. "It's been a long time. I'm not a kid anymore. I don't know why I'm so upset over it."

For a while, neither of them spoke, just watched the snow fall faster around them. Then Joe said quietly, "There's one more thing I didn't tell you about yourself."

She turned, blinked at him.

"You're beautiful, Anne Macy."

Annie's throat tightened and a myriad of emotions she couldn't begin to name swirled inside of her. Unable to speak, she drank in the sight of his tough, handsome face…

Minutes passed. Everything that had happened since last night caught up to her and Annie's eyelids grew heavy. She yawned.

"Why don't you crawl in back and catch some shut-eye?" Joe said.

"I should stay awake and talk to you so you won't drift off at that wheel."

"I'm used to running on a few hours' sleep."

Annie lifted her head. "If the roads aren't too bad when I wake up, I'll drive while you sleep, okay?"

"Sounds like a deal."

Minutes later, curled up in the back seat beneath Harry's coat, Annie said, "My mother...everyone has always said I'm like her. That used to make me so proud. But now..." She sighed. "Mom wasn't always unhappy. I always miss her most this time of year...at Christmas, you know? She always made it so special."

"How so, Annie?"

"She always had us sing carols while we decorated the tree and the house. The fun carols, not the serious ones. And she changed the words, made them funnier, sillier. And the entire month of December, she'd hide little notes all over the house. She rolled them up into tiny scrolls and tied them with ribbons. They'd say things like, 'Good for one afternoon of cookie decorating', or 'Good for one midnight drive to see the Christmas lights'."

"Sounds like fun."

She thought back for a minute on all the Christmases they'd spent together. "My best memory, though, it happened when I was ten or eleven. Mom and I were dressed up to go to a holiday tea on a Saturday afternoon. It was snowing and I just wanted to stay home. I hated those things and I had complained all morning, but people were expecting us." Annie paused for a breath. "As we were pulling out of the driveway, the sun came out and without saying a word, Mom stopped the car and got out. I rolled down my window to ask what was going on, and she threw a snowball at me." Annie laughed. "We never made it to that tea. We spent the rest of the afternoon having snowball fights and sledding and making snowmen." She opened her eyes. "I've never forgotten that day. I loved every minute of it. I can still hear her laughing. She had the greatest laugh."

"So do you," Joe said. "That's one way you're like her."

Her throat ached. "Thank you for saying that."

Snow swirled outside the car window. Annie's eyelids became heavier. She hoped her mother had always remembered that wonderful day, too. And that it had meant as much to her.

CHAPTER 9

Joe tugged open the car door and slid behind the wheel. He was glad he had thought to bring gloves before he left the apartment. If they had to dig out, he didn't relish the thought of doing it bare-handed. With a shudder, he dusted snow off his jacket, then pulled the gloves off and turned. Annie was awake now. Tangled blond hair brushed her shoulders. Her sleepy eyes watched him. The desire he'd been fighting all day slammed into him like a two-ton brick.

"Is something wrong?" she asked.

Oh, yeah, he thought. Plenty was wrong, and the worst of it had nothing to do with the weather. "We're stuck." He tossed the gloves onto the passenger seat.

She sat up. "What happened?"

"I think we were being followed. I was afraid Willis might have caught up to us when we stopped to grab a bite." They'd pulled off at a diner for lunch earlier, and when he had not let Annie drive afterward, she'd fallen asleep again. "I tried to lose the vehicle by taking a detour and ended up here." *Here* being nose-down in a ditch on a deserted farm road in the middle of nowhere.

"Oh." Annie stared outside into the white chaos that swarmed in the gathering darkness beyond the windows. "Did you lose the car that was following us?"

"For now," he answered. At least she didn't berate him for doing something so stupid as pulling off the main highway during a blizzard. If their positions were reversed, Joe wasn't sure he'd be so kind.

Shivering, Annie huddled deeper into Landau's coat. "It's so dark. How long have I slept?"

"About three hours. It's after seven."

"The blizzard seems worse."

"I thought about walking to the last little town we passed through. It's not far, but I'm not sure I could see two feet in front of me."

"That's a terrible idea. It's too dangerous. You could get lost out there and freeze to death. Someone will drive by and help us."

"I wouldn't count on that. Not on this road with the weather like it is."

Her frown deepened. "Do you have any idea where we are?"

"According to the map, we were getting close to your aunt's place."

She sighed. "What now?"

"You take the wheel, and I'll try to push us out."

Ten minutes later, Joe gave up. Their efforts had only dug

the tires deeper into the snowbank. He instructed Annie to turn off the engine and give him the key. Then he trudged around back and opened the trunk where he kept a blanket. He'd never been a Boy Scout but when it came to safety, his police training had taught him to always be prepared.

Panting from exertion and the cold, he slid in and closed the door. Annie had climbed up front into the passenger-side bucket seat. He lifted the blanket between them for her to see. "I'm afraid we have a long, cold night ahead of us."

Her gaze strayed to the frosted window where the wind whistled and howled. Then she gave him a sleepy-eyed smile. "I'm not worried. We Georgia girls know how to generate heat." With a nod of her head, she motioned toward the back seat. "We should get out of these bucket seats and in back so we can share body warmth." She shifted to crawl between the seats.

Joe knew she was right; sharing body warmth would be the smart thing to do. He also knew she was trying to make the best of a bad situation with all that lighthearted talk about "Georgia girls." But he wasn't fooled. Annie was as conflicted as he was about crawling into that back seat together.

He'd meant it earlier when he said she didn't seem the type to have flings. But Joe had also noticed the way she studied him sometimes. When they looked at each other, he wasn't the only one who liked what he saw. Still, he was pretty sure Annie was giving priority to rationality rather than sexuality by inviting him into the back seat with her.

But he wasn't certain he could do the same with her beside him all night long.

After a tormenting back-and-forth with himself, Joe finally joined her.

Annie ran a hand across Harry Landau's coat. "This is big enough for both of us to cover up with."

"Right now, I'm pretty thankful to the poor creature who gave up its life so Landau could look pretentious," Joe said. He reached over into the front and retrieved the blanket, his pulse kicking up as they unfolded it together. Shifting, they spread it across the seat. He willed himself to behave like a responsible adult as Annie shrugged out of Landau's coat then pulled off her boots.

"Nice argyles," he said, teasing her about her wool socks.

"My feet are like ice blocks all winter. I have a feeling my proper southern ancestors have turned over in their graves a time or two because of me."

"Argyles are a crime?"

She fluttered her eyelashes dramatically. "A proper southern lady always looks her best, doesn't blow her nose in public and absolutely never, ever sweats."

Laughing, Joe eyed the narrow seat, wondering how he would ever get any sleep with Annie stretched out so close to him. "How do you want to do this?" he asked her.

"Why don't you lay with your back to the seat, and I'll lay with my back to you?"

He didn't have to look down at his lap to know that

having her backside pressed against his frontside was not a good idea. "I'm kind of claustrophobic. You mind if we switch that up?"

"No, that's fine."

Annie stretched out, and Joe lay down on the seat beside her, teetering on the edge, facing the front of the car. He pulled the coat over them both.

She draped an arm across his waist.

He felt her breasts press against his back.

"This isn't going to work," she said with a sigh. "Our heads are downhill."

The position of their heads was the least of Joe's concerns. Still he said, "Let's turn around then." He sat up, scooted to the opposite end of the seat, perched at the edge.

Annie lifted her feet, swung them to the floorboard, held onto the coat and scooted down beside him. "Sorry to be such a pain. You must think I'm high-maintenance."

Joe stared straight ahead, afraid if she saw his face, she'd read what was on his mind. "Not high-maintenance, just uncomfortable."

"I'm not." She cleared her throat. Cleared it again. "Uncomfortable, I mean. I'm not, Joe."

He felt her breath on his cheek and turned, met her wide gaze.

"*Joe*," she whispered.

In that instant, every argument about why this was a bad idea dislodged from Joe's brain and began to fly out his ears along with his good sense. He kissed her, leaned his head forward slightly and gently touched his mouth to hers. Her lips weren't cold at all. They were warmer and softer than he had even imagined. He deepened the kiss, tasted her, and her quiet moan wrapped around him and squeezed. Coming up for air, he murmured, "Annie."

Anne. Annabelle Macy. Macy, as in, Milford P.

Jesus, what was he doing?

Joe tensed and leaned away suddenly, caught hold of the last thread-thin remnants of his self-restraint before they exited his brain, too. He reached for the coat on the seat beside them. Time to put an end to this before it went too far.

"Here. Cover up," he croaked.

Annie caught his gaze, held it. "I think what we were doing was a much better way to stay warm," she said in a throaty voice that turned him upside down and inside out.

Before he could think of a rational response, she reached up and grasped his shoulders, slid sideways onto his lap and kissed him softly again, just once, before easing back to look at him.

His last thread of sanity snapped apart. Joe pulled her closer, tangled his fingers through her hair, tilted her face up. This time, he didn't dip gently toward her mouth, he *dove*. And before he knew how it happened or who initiated the move, she was straddling his lap and they sat face-to-face with her knees pressed gently at either side of his hips. They stopped kissing and blinked at each other.

"Annie…are you sure about this?" He tucked a strand of hair behind her ear. His heart bounced around in his chest like a pinball. Smiling, Joe asked quietly, "Doesn't it break some kind of proper southern belle rule?"

She smiled back. "I've never been a very good southern belle, anyway." She unzipped his jacket and reached for the hem of his T-shirt.

"Annie…I'm no different than those losers from your past. Only with a lot less to offer."

"Don't say that. It's not true." She shook her head. "Please don't ask me to think twice about this. I don't care if it's crazy. I've imagined being with you since you dropped my purse last night and I opened the bathroom door. Maybe before then. The way you look at me…" She averted her eyes briefly, met his gaze again. "I don't think I've ever been with a man who wanted to make love with me just because…" Her brows tugged together and she looked down.

"Because you're beautiful? Exasperating and sexy and vital and—?" Joe frowned. "A man would have to be crazy not to see those things."

She met his gaze again and the desire in her eyes sucked the breath from Joe's lungs. Suddenly, he couldn't move, couldn't breathe. *He* wanted her. For all those reasons and more. The rational, professional side of him screamed *no. Big mistake.* But the part of him that was simply a man— not an ex-cop, not a private investigator—screamed louder. And it screamed *yes.* He wanted her more than his own self-respect. More than the money her father owed him. More than he wanted Frank Reno's head on a plate. He wanted to show her just how special she was, prove to her that all men were not like the idiots from her past, make her feel the way she deserved to feel. He swallowed again. "I don't have any protection with me."

She sent him a hesitant smile. "Can you reach my purse?"

He leaned over, felt along the floorboard until he found it. "I forgot about your stash. You want to explain that, by the way?"

"It was a gag gift from Lacy at the Christmas party last night." Annie took the purse from him, opened it. "Private joke. She thinks I'm a nun in disguise. Lacy's forever trying to 'get me some action,' as she puts it."

Joe kept his eyes on her as she placed a condom packet on the dash behind them. God, she was something else. Not even close to what he'd expected when he took this case. His nerves hummed and his heart drummed a wild beat when she slid her hands under his shirt and up to his bare chest.

He had convinced himself he could resist her, told himself he didn't have any other choice. From the moment she climbed in his cab for the first time last night, he had known that being with her like this would mess with his mind, make him so crazy he couldn't think straight, place them both in more danger than they already faced.

He was a grown man with a lot of years behind him, not some testosterone-crazed kid. But with her sweet round bottom settled atop his lap, her soft breasts pressing against the smooth fabric of her satin blouse, and her vulnerable expression twisting him up inside, Joe felt all those initial good intentions peeling away like old paint.

He swept hair from her face, cradled her cheek in his hand. "Be sure, Annie. Once we start this—"

"Shhh." Smiling, she touched a finger to his lips. "Too late. We've already started."

He let her help him out of his coat and shirt then tossed them to the floor of the car. "I love the way you smell," he whispered, taking hold of her shoulders and drawing her against him. "So sweet…" He nipped gently at her lips, teasing, tasting, then deepened the kiss, skimming his palms up satin from her waist to the swell of her breasts.

When she moaned quietly into his mouth, he inched farther down in the seat, reached for the hem of her skirt, tugged it up around her waist and grasped hold of her hips. With his fingers pressed against the silky panties covering her bottom, he forgot the cold and the blustering storm outside, forgot their precarious situation and everything else except Annie and his own driving need.

"Joe…I…" She fumbled with his belt buckle.

He helped her unclasp it, slid his zipper down, brushed his knuckles against her inner thighs. She arched her back in a way that thrust her breasts closer to his face. "God," Joe breathed, "look at you. Lift your arms for me, Annie."

She did, and he pulled the shirt over her head, then

fumbled with the bra clasp between her breasts. She reached up to help him and their gazes collided, held. Their fingers bumped. Annie's breathless laughter scattered goose bumps up his spine.

Finally, the bra came free and Joe whisked it off and looked at her. "You're more than I ever dreamed, Annie. So much more. So beautiful," Joe said, his voice a low smooth rumble that rolled through her like thunder, shaking her. He leaned forward and kissed her, cupping her breasts in his hands, caressing and teasing, sending a rush of pleasure through her so intense she almost stopped breathing.

Lowering one hand to her panties, he slid his fingers inside and stroked her until she begged him not to stop.

"Wait, honey," he whispered, then he leaned back, said, "Lift up a second. Let me get out of these jeans."

Annie moved to one side and slipped off her clothes while he shoved his jeans and briefs to his ankles. In only seconds, he was out of them. She drank in the sight and feel of him from his beautiful eyes all the way down. Incredible. Gorgeous. There weren't enough words to describe what she thought of him. She loved looking at his broad shoulders, the dark dusting of hair on his chest, his flat stomach. He was every inch male, every inch beautiful, so blatantly sexy she almost couldn't breathe.

He pulled her onto his lap again. She held her breath as she looked down, blinked and stared, then met Joe's gaze with an appreciative smile. His dark eyes gleamed, and when she touched him, his quick intake of breath only encouraged her. Annie imagined what he would feel like inside of her, filling her, moving, easing the mindless unbearable ache between her thighs.

"Tell me what you want, Annie. Tell me what you imagined last night."

When she did, he reached back with one hand, and then he was tearing into the small packet that held the condom. Seconds later, he leaned her against the fur coat and settled himself between her legs, holding his body slightly above her with his arms.

Annie heard the hiss of the wind, felt the car rock and sway and a tiny draft of cold air at the edge of the door. The brush of Joe's chest tickled her breasts, making her nerve endings sing, her stomach clamp tight, the yearning spread. Then there was only his weight on top of her, his mouth at her breast, sucking and soothing, a hot rush of pleasure as he thrust inside of her.

She wrapped her legs around his waist, rocked against him, matching the rhythm he'd started, losing herself in the sounds and scents and sensations of their lovemaking. Sighs and moans and murmured words, Joe's musky smell mingling with her own, his hands and mouth everywhere, building an overwhelming pressure within her that grew and grew until she thought she'd scream. And his eyes…they looked down at her…dark and hot and heart-stopping.

"Let go, Annie," Joe said in a low voice. "It's just you and me."

And then she did scream, closed her eyes and cried out as spasms tore through her body with a shattering force. She held on to him, felt his shoulders tense, felt his answering shudder of release before he went lax on top of her.

They clung to each other as they spiraled back down, and when Annie could think again, she was in total awe of what had just happened, the way he'd made her feel with a perfect combination of tenderness and passion. When Joe touched her, kissed her, looked at her, he convinced her she was all those things he'd proclaimed her to be. Beautiful. Sexy and exasperating. Vital. She smiled lazily, amazed. He'd said she was 'vital'. Who knew how sexy that description would be? How much she'd needed to hear it?

Joe had known. He'd *known*.

"Joe…I never—"

"Me, either." He lifted a hand, stroked her hair. "Not like that. Never like that."

Annie laughed. "Joe?"

"Hmmm?"

"If we get out of this mess alive, remind me to thank Lacy for her Christmas gift, would you?"

"Only if you thank her for me, too."

He lifted his head, smiled down at her with heavy-lidded eyes.

And just like that, Annie felt it, that elusive, mysterious

zing Sara had described. That feeling in the pit of her stomach that told her she just *had to have this man,* that she wouldn't survive if she ever had to let him go.

CHAPTER 10

Annie lay with her ear against Joe's chest, listening to his heartbeat. She was naked and warm stretched out on top of him now, beneath Harry's coat. Except for her nose. Her nose was numb. She scooted up, nuzzled her face into the crook of Joe's neck.

He played with her hair while his other hand rubbed the small of her back, her hip, her bottom. They hadn't said much for the past half hour, just held one another. Annie was half afraid to speak. Too many words might break the spell, the simple perfection of what had happened between them.

"My feet are warm," she said finally. "They're never warm. Not in the winter. It's a miracle."

"I have that effect on women." Joe's voice was a low rasp in the darkness. "We should get dressed before the heat wears off."

She lifted her head and smiled down at him. "I think we have a while before that happens."

He traced a fingertip down her jawline, touched her lower lip, lingered. "I'm having a hard time figuring out why all your fiancés let you slip away."

"Oh, they didn't want to. But the truth is, I don't think they were really after me. They were after the fringe benefits that came *with* me. Did I tell you my father's filthy, stinking rich?"

He didn't answer that question, just watched her, twisting a lock of her hair around his finger. "I think you sell yourself short. How do you know it was only the money they wanted?"

She shrugged. "They were all considered good catches, you know? They could've had their pick of women who would've been happy to stay home and run a household and entertain, and all that. And then, with the last two, I was older by then. Chuck and Lance had plenty of twenty-somethings panting at their heels. Why else would they have chosen me?"

Joe sent her a bemused narrow-eyed look. "Who wants a girl when they can have a full-grown woman?" He squeezed her bottom.

"It doesn't matter," Annie said with a laugh. "I didn't want *them*." She looked into his eyes. "They weren't my type. I realize that now."

The moonlight reflecting off the snow illuminated Joe's face. Annie touched her lips to the discolored skin beneath his left eye where she'd hit him with her shoe during the scuffle in her apartment. In the space of an instant, he had gone from satisfied and smiling, to troubled. She could feel it, see it in his expression, sense the sudden tension in him.

She shifted a bit to her side, lifted onto her elbow.

He glanced away.

Why had she said that? Insinuated that *he* was her type. Obviously, Joe wasn't ready to take what they'd started a step further. Maybe he never would be. He hadn't promised her anything. She shouldn't take it for granted that had had felt what she did when they'd made love.

"I don't expect anything from you, Joe. I understand if what just happened didn't mean anything."

"It meant something, Annie. This shaky self-image thing you have goin' on—"

"I don't have a shaky self-image," she protested, but she thought to herself, he *can* see right through me.

Joe scowled at her. "You told me people have always said you're like your mother. Are you afraid that's true?"

Annie averted her gaze. "Before I found out the truth—" She sighed, looked at him again. "I used to think they were paying me a compliment, or at least I convinced myself of that. If I'm honest, though, I think I always knew there was a different side to her, that she had problems. But I didn't want to hear it or admit it any more than my father wanted to tell me." She shook her head, huffed a humorless laugh. "I guess I'm just as guilty of keeping myself in the dark about my mother as he is."

"You've told me some great things about her…"

"And some not so great things."

"But it's those good things you mentioned that I see in you. Her laughter. The times when she was happy, when she put you and your dad first and made things special."

Annie felt tears of gratitude gathering behind her eyes. It was so hard…loving her mother, wanting to be proud of her, but doubting her, too.

"My dad," he continued. "After my brother was killed and Pop lost himself, I had to keep reminding myself of the way he was before he started drinking too much and gambling away every penny he made. I had to hold onto the memories of the father and husband he was when I was growing up. I knew that man was still inside him." Joe paused, added, "I think it's the same with you and your mother."

She brushed her knuckles against his beard-stubbled cheek. "There you go again, ruining your tough-guy image by being sweet."

Joe slid his hand to the nape of her neck and pressed her head down toward his until their mouths touched. Still, Annie sensed conflict in him.

"What are you thinking?" she asked.

"I don't want to hurt you, Annie. No matter what happens—"

"My eyes were wide open going into this. They still are. I don't expect anything," she repeated.

But she wanted it. Oh, how she wanted it.

Joe didn't look at her.

Desperate to lighten his mood, Annie tilted her head to one side and said, "Do you realize we've known one another less than twenty-four hours?" She smirked at him. "And you thought I was a prude. Now, I suppose you think I'm a loose woman."

He laughed. "Yeah, and I love it."

"After what we just did, you may find this hard to believe, but being naughty *is* a whole new experience for me."

"And you chose me to help guide you down the path to corruption. How'd I get so lucky?"

"You looked as if you'd be good at it."

"And what do you think so far? Am I measuring up?"

She nuzzled his ear with her mouth, felt him harden against her thigh. "Oh, you definitely *measure up*. I had a very good time." She giggled. "Next time, that is if you're *up* to it—"

He closed his eyes.

Gawd. Why couldn't she stop saying the wrong things? Maybe he intended this to be a one-time incident. "I only want sex from you, Brady," she said, trying to tease him out of his funk. "I'm not asking for your soul, just this." Annie slipped her hand between their bodies and touched him. "I promise I'll return it in the same condition I found it in."

Joe groaned. "Sweet Tea, after tonight it's never gonna be the same."

Laughing, Annie propped a forearm against Joe's chest and trailed the fingers of her opposite hand down a jagged scar that stretched like a tiny lightning bolt from his collarbone to his shoulder. "What happened here?"

"Knife wound."

She flinched, stunned by his indifferent tone. "Did it happen in the line of duty or during your wayward youth?"

"Line of duty. When you work undercover, sometimes it goes with the territory."

"Can you tell me about it?"

His eyes remained closed. "We should sleep."

"I'm not sleepy. I slept while you drove."

"Well, I am." After a moment, he opened his eyes, and when he found her staring down at him expectantly, Joe exhaled noisily. "Okay. I'll tell you, but then you've gotta let me get some sleep."

"Deal." She balanced her forearms on his chest.

Joe waited a few beats, then said, "It helps to be a good liar when you work undercover. If you screw up and they call your bluff, you might wind up in the E.R. or worse. I screwed up."

"How?"

"I was posing as a customer trying to buy cocaine. The dealer was a cop. That academy classmate of Willis's I mentioned. I'd met with him before under an assumed name to arrange things. This particular time, though, he brought a friend, and it just so happened the guy knew me."

"You mean he knew you were a cop?"

Joe nodded. "I got a little cut up, but it was worth it. That wasn't the first time I took in a crooked cop. Wasn't the last time, either. Which is why I developed a reputation that didn't set well with a few of my fellow officers."

"I don't understand their way of thinking. They should've applauded you."

"I don't get it, either. Most cops don't. It's hard enough dealing with the criminals on the outside without being forced to deal with them inside the ranks, too."

Annie studied him. "Why did you do it if you knew they'd come down on you?"

"I was good at it."

Annie caught a hint of something cold and bitter in his expression as she traced the scar. She sensed more to the wound than what she could see. As he sifted through his thoughts, it occurred to her that they might as well have existed on different planets before they met. Her run-in with Harry Landau last night was the closest she had ever come to touching the darker side of life.

"I told you about my little brother," Joe finally said. "He was an addict by the time he turned fourteen. When he was in junior high, the neighborhood we lived in was really starting to go downhill. So it was no big surprise he got mixed up with a gang. A lot of kids did."

He shook his head. "Ma tried to talk my dad into moving out of the neighborhood to a safer place, but Pop grew up there and he had the attitude that he wasn't going to let any scumbags scare him away from his home."

"I can understand him feeling that way," Annie said.

"I do, too. But it's not easy keeping a kid straight in that atmosphere. Once they're caught up in the culture…" He shrugged. "When you get right down to it, my brother was just another statistic."

"Don't say that."

His jaw clamped tight. "After Pete died, they arrested his gang's supplier. A patrol officer who worked our neighborhood. A guy everybody looked up to. I guess that's part of the reason that I chose to work narcotics. Because of my brother."

Because he'd wanted revenge, like she did for her mother. No wonder Joe understood her so well.

"I didn't hesitate to go after guys who used their badge for the wrong reasons."

Lowering her head, she kissed the thick white mark that pocked his chest. "It must've been horrible for you and your parents, losing your brother like that."

"I was old enough to see where he was headed. I should've done something."

"Nineteen is still a boy, Joe. A boy can't be expected to save the world."

He didn't respond, and in the short silence that followed she thought of the woman who had been attacked on his guard, an incident he obviously blamed on himself. "Neither can a grown man," she said. "You aren't responsible for everyone, Joe."

He closed his eyes again. "I know that."

Annie laid her head on his chest. After awhile, she felt Joe relax and he began rubbing her back. She didn't believe him. He *did* feel responsible. Even for her. "You're not responsible for me, either," she said quietly.

His hands stilled, and after a long stretch of silence, he said, "What happened between us tonight...you may not believe it right now, but you'll probably regret it some day. When that day comes, you'll hate me."

She flinched, lifted her head. "I could never hate you. Why would you say that?"

He cradled her face between his palms, scattered kisses across her eyes, her cheeks, her lips. "I couldn't stand it if you got hurt because of me, Annie. I couldn't stand for you to hate me."

"I won't get hurt," she whispered, her throat closing. The hopelessness in his tone, the inevitability, frightened her. "Be with me because you want to, not because you think I can't take care of myself. I've dealt with that enough all my life."

He wrapped his arms around her, held her. "Let's get some sleep. We have a long day ahead tomorrow."

Annie sighed, caught between the contentment she felt in Joe's arms and the worry his words inspired. "I don't want to think about tomorrow. I just want you to hold me."

THE DISTANT BUZZ of a motor stirred Joe to consciousness. He tried moving his hand but couldn't feel it. And then he remembered...Annie.

Joe opened his eyes. Sunlight filtered through the snow-encrusted window. The glass sparkled like a sheet of tiny diamonds. When he moved, Annie moaned quietly against him. He reached down and felt on the floor for his clothes.

"Annie, I think someone's coming. We'd better get dressed."

Yawning, she tugged the coat to her chin and sat up, her hair forming a pale, tangled halo around her sleep-lined face. She blinked, then widened her eyes. "Willis?"

"I doubt it's him." Joe twisted his legs around and sat up. "If he followed us off the exit, he probably got stuck, too."

They dressed in a hurry, hastened by the biting cold as well as the vehicle's approach. Joe put on his gloves then reached over the seat for his coat. He put it on, too, then tried to open the door. It had frozen shut and he had to use his shoulder to give it a few hard shoves. Finally, the door gave way and he stepped outside into a three-foot snowdrift.

Joe trudged up the incline and out of the ditch as a blue pickup truck slowed to a stop at the road's edge. The driver's window rolled down and an old man with sagging jowls and an orange stocking hat with a fluffy round puff on top of it looked out. "Hey, buddy," the old man said. "Looks like you could use some help."

"Sure could." Joe approached the truck. The wind had died down, but the temperature still felt like ten below. "Is that a four-wheel drive?"

The man nodded. "Yessir, and I've got chains. I'll pull you out of there, no problem."

The elderly man left the truck idling while he climbed

out. He was overweight, with friendly gray eyes and a firm handshake. "Name's Nate Kilroy. You're lucky I came along," he said, whistling softly as he talked. "This road isn't traveled much."

Joe introduced himself, then followed Nate's gaze toward the GTO where Annie was climbing onto the road.

"You two spend the night out here?"

"We did, sir," Annie answered, shoving her hands into the pockets of Landau's coat. "I wouldn't recommend it." Her eyes flicked to Joe a second as she smiled and added, "We managed to stay warm enough, but you're still a sight for sore eyes."

They exchanged introductions, then Nate hauled a coil of chains from the bed of his truck.

Joe pulled out his wallet, noted his cash was dwindling fast, then said, "Will ten bucks pay for your trouble?"

The old man scowled at him, then turned and spit onto the road. "No charge. I hope someone would do the same for me."

Fifteen minutes later, Joe's GTO was out of the ditch and Annie was getting directions to her aunt's place from Nate. After saying their goodbyes, Annie and Joe climbed into the car. "We're only minutes away from Aunt Tess's," Annie said, waving at Nate as they passed by his truck.

Joe glanced into the mirror, noting that the old man followed closely behind them. "Nice old guy."

"Yes." Annie laughed softly. "He needs new dentures. They whistle." She leaned across the space between the seats that separated them, brought her mouth up to Joe's ear and murmured, "One of Aunt Tess's bedrooms has a fireplace and a bed so big you could get lost in it." She nibbled his lobe, and added, "Why don't we get lost in it together once we're there? My feet are getting cold again."

"I'm starting to think you have as much of a one-track mind as I do."

She grinned up at him and unzipped his coat. "Is that a problem?"

"Not as long as we're on the same track." Desire twisted inside him again as she slipped her hand beneath his shirt-tail. "I need some nourishment first if I'm going to keep up with you."

"Maybe Aunt Tess has some canned goods in the pantry." She poked her finger into his navel.

Joe jumped. "Jesus, Annie! I'm going to slide off the road again if you don't behave yourself. Move on over to your side and buckle up."

Her laugh skittered goose bumps up his arms. "You're no fun."

"I wasn't hearing any complaints out of you last night."

Joe gripped the wheel, his mind in turmoil. He couldn't think of anything better than a day spent in a real bed with Annie. But he couldn't do that with a clear conscience unless he told her the truth about himself. And that was the problem. In bed with him was the last place she'd want to be when she found out he was really an investigator working for her father, when she realized that he'd kept that from her long after he should've. As it stood, he could either satisfy his conscience or satisfy his lust. For the life of him, he couldn't figure out a way to do both.

Annie nuzzled his neck, and Joe bit the inside of his cheek. Hard. What did it matter? When the truth came out, Annie was going to be hurt and pissed off whether he slept with her again or not. She had implied she just wanted sex with him, no strings. If that was the case, the truth should-n't make any difference.

His self-serving rationalizations disgusted him. First of all, he didn't believe her. He'd been right; Annie wasn't the type of woman who had flings. If he'd been thinking straight last night, he would've respected that, realized what he was setting himself up for and backed off.

"You're quiet," Annie murmured.

"Just tired," he said. "Someone kept me up last night."

Joe flexed his fingers on the wheel, shifted in his seat. If he wanted to hang onto his one last shred of self-respect, he had to tell Annie the truth. He would remind her that he hadn't known her when he made that deal with her father. He had just been doing a job, following orders. When she thought about that, she would be fine. He tried to convince himself that was possible. He'd lay it all out rationally, she'd listen, and like a reasonable adult, she'd understand. The air would clear and they could get down to the business of wading through those files while enjoying one another's company.

"Annie?"

"Mmm-hmm?" she answered drowsily.

"Does your aunt's place have a phone?"

"I think so. Why?"

"We should probably let our families know we're okay."

She sighed. "You're right. Daddy's probably been sitting by the phone all night."

Joe felt a sudden case of indigestion coming on. Through the rearview mirror, he saw Nate take the cut-off into town. He waved at the old man and stayed on the road Annie told him to follow. "About your father—"

"Oh, look!" Annie pointed out the front window. "There's the house. See?"

It wasn't a house, it was a barn. A big, red barn at the edge of a snowy meadow adorned with a scattering of trees and a frozen pond perfect for ice-skating. The sight seemed familiar. Joe pondered that, and realized he had seen it on at least a hundred Christmas cards. "Where's the house?"

"The barn *is* the house. It's been converted. Wait until you see inside of it. Tess left the beams exposed and had wood plank floors installed. It's full of antiques, and besides that bedroom I told you about, there's an enormous great room with another fireplace." She squeezed his arm. "After we call our folks, I'll give you a tour. Then we can scrounge up some food."

Joe's stomach growled. He decided the truth would have to wait until after they ate. Yesterday, he'd witnessed Annie's temper. Joe knew he couldn't face the full force of it on an empty belly. He saw what she did to that three-hundred-pound gorilla back at her apartment. He was going to need his strength.

For just a moment, his thoughts drifted to the bedroom with the fireplace. He reined them in. First, calls home. Second, food. Then the truth. No excuses. After that, if he was lucky…

PACIFYING HER FATHER was no simple task. Annie understood his worries. She even felt guilty about causing them. By getting involved with Harry Landau, she had pulled her father back into the past. He was reliving what had happened to her mom so long ago, and terrified that his worst nightmare might be coming true—that he might lose his daughter like he had his wife. As upset as Annie was with him, her intentions when she took a job with Harry had never been to hurt her father.

"He wants to talk to you again," Annie said, passing the phone to Joe. When he took it, she added, "I'm going to take a quick shower before we eat. Feel free to join me when you're finished with Daddy."

He didn't. In fact, when she went looking for him after her shower, she heard water spraying in the bathroom next door to the one she had occupied. She tried the door and found it locked.

Baffled and a little hurt, Annie walked barefoot down the hallway to the bedroom she hoped they would share. She loved the feel of the polished plank floor beneath her feet, loved the splashes of color in the rugs and pillows and throws Aunt Tess had scattered everywhere. The house was decorated for comfort and relaxation. A perfect place for lovers.

In Tess's closet, she was surprised to find an assortment of lingerie, from elegant to gaudy with every style in between. Annie was aware that her aunt periodically entertained guests here. Now she wondered if those guests were men. The thought made Annie smile. Tess loved the opposite sex and made no effort to hide the fact.

A thought struck her again, and her smile fell away. Had her mother entertained lovers, too? Was Frank Reno one of them? While the prospect of Tess's risqué love life pleased and amused her, the possibility of her mother's did not. Tess had no commitments to anyone. Lydia had had a husband and child who loved her. Did her mother betray them both?

Annie felt a subtle shift in her anger toward her father. He had tried so hard to maintain her mother's good memory. Annie wasn't so sure that Lydia deserved his efforts. But then it occurred to her that he hadn't done it for her mother. He had done it for *her*. So that she could feel proud of the woman who had brought her into the world and raised her. Annie had only known her mother sixteen years, but she had known her father for forty. She had no doubts at all that he was a good man who always had her best interest at heart, even if that interest was sometimes misguided. She no longer had that same certainty about her mother.

Annie continued looking through Tess's closet. She

might never have the answers she sought. Maybe they had died along with her mother.

The robe Annie chose wasn't Tess's most conservative nor her most revealing. The burgundy satin clung to every curve, leaving little to the imagination. Tying the sash around her waist, Annie stepped back and scrutinized her image in the mirror. *Not bad for middle-aged.* She felt young, as young and alive as she had ever felt.

In the kitchen pantry, she found tins of caviar, jars of pickled vegetables and olives. Bottled water sat on a refrigerator shelf, and a huge selection of wine filled a rack that covered half of one wall. After filling a tray, she made her way down the hall toward the bedrooms again. When she passed by the room where Joe had showered, she heard him talking on the telephone again.

Seconds later, in the large bedroom, she placed the tray on the rug in front of the fireplace hearth then went to see if the bed needed linens. Her aunt didn't fail her. Tess always made a point of leaving the place ready for the next group of guests. Plump pillows lay scattered across the headboard of the huge four-poster bed. Annie grabbed several and tossed them on the rug beside the tray.

Soon, Joe appeared in the doorway. She planted her hands on her hips. "I was beginning to think you might be avoiding me."

"I talked to my mother. She went to stay with Ed and Nancy Simms like I wanted her to."

"No complaints?"

"Nope. A million questions, though."

"Must be nice," Annie said with no little amount of sarcasm, thinking of her conversation with her father.

"I tried to get ahold of my old partner, O'Malley, too. Got his machine again. I left him this number." His gaze swept down the front of her robe, her bare legs and feet. He shoved fingers through his damp hair and the ends curled slightly when his hand came away.

"I see you showered, too." She stuck out her lower lip, her pout only half in jest. "You locked me out."

He wore the same jeans he'd worn in the car. No shirt. His feet were bare. He seemed more real, more imposing in the daylight, less like a fantasy. Flesh and bone and muscle. Hard angles. Masculine heat.

Last night came to her in a flash. The feel of his body, his scent, the taste of his breath and skin. Her heart took off on a chaotic chase. She was in over her head. Crazy about him. The way he looked and talked, the way he moved, the way he made love. Everything about Joe Brady got to her, made her ache with an edgy need. She felt it again, that *zing* Sara had mentioned. It seemed impossible, insane, after knowing him such a short time, that she was in love with him.

And not just with his physical assets, either. She loved his tough strength, his tender heart, his belief in justice. She loved that he loved his mother and let her baby him, even though she sensed the woman sometimes drove him crazy. She loved that he ached for the father and brother he had lost. That he could see straight into her heart and soul and mind and understand what he found there better than anyone else ever had.

Joe Brady was a very good man. They'd been through a lot in a short time. And Annie didn't need to know him one second longer to know that she loved him.

"Sorry I locked the door." Joe sat on the floor and reached for the jar of olives. He slanted her a smug look and said, "I guess I'm shy."

"Since when?" she scoffed, and sat beside him.

"Since I decided we'd never get around to eating if we showered together." His gaze skimmed the front of her robe again. She wore nothing beneath it and she knew that was obvious. Joe's throat bobbed. He looked away.

Frustration swept through her. Why had the tone between them changed? He was holding back, pulling away from her.

"You shaved," she said.

"Yeah. I found a razor in the medicine cabinet. Must've belonged to your aunt's really old boyfriend."

Or one of her new ones, Annie thought smugly.

"I was thinking," Joe said as he set the olive jar aside unopened. "Maybe I should take a look at the files now, see if I can spot something you missed."

"We have plenty of time for that. Harry won't find us here."

"We shouldn't put it off. We—"

"Did my father say something to scare you away from me?"

His flinch was subtle and quick. "No, why?"

"Before you talked to him, you were more interested in me than in the files."

"Aren't you ready to get to the bottom of this?"

"Yes, I'm anxious. But I'm anxious to do some other things, too. Such as…" Annie leaned over and whispered in his ear.

Joe's brows shot up. He blinked at her, cleared his throat, lifted a tin of caviar and said, "I've never had caviar."

A slap of humiliation stung her cheeks. He regretted last night. That's what this was all about. He didn't want her.

Out of nowhere, the memory of the look of longing Lance and the wedding planner had shared, of finding them together only minutes before she and Lance were supposed to become man and wife, rushed back to Annie, bringing insecurities she didn't know she possessed. She had convinced herself that because she hadn't really loved Lance, his betrayal hadn't affected her. But now the hurt feelings and self-doubts she'd suppressed surged over her like a tidal wave, sucking her under.

"Annie," Joe said with a tinge of nervousness in his tone, "We need to talk."

She stood abruptly, knocking over the olive jar, embarrassed and disgusted with herself for wearing the revealing robe. Crossing her arms over her breasts, she walked to the dresser and leaned against it, unable to meet her own gaze in the mirror. "You don't need to explain. I misunderstood. After last night, I just—" Her voice caught. She was making an even bigger fool of herself. Annie wished she could shrink, slither beneath the rug like a worm. "I guess I should've paid more attention to what Lance and the wedding planner were trying to tell me."

"Annie." Joe was behind her so fast that the touch of his hands on her shoulders startled her. "It's nothing like that. I want you so much I can't breathe." He pressed his face into her hair. His fingertips brushed her collarbone. "You deserve someone better than me."

"Why do you keep saying that?" Her voice faltered again. "Why is it so hard for everyone to let me decide what's best for me? I'm a full-grown woman. I know what I want." She lifted her head, met his gaze in the mirror. "I want to be with you, Joe. If you don't want to be with me, say so now and I'll accept it. But if you do…" She blinked at him, took a breath. "If you do, stop questioning it."

CHAPTER 11

God, yes, he wanted to be with her.

Joe's conversation with Milford Macy hadn't changed that fact. But it had caused him to take a step back and remember he was here to work a case, not to have his way with the old man's daughter.

Macy's concerns about Annie's safety had also brought back that promise Joe had made to himself after Emma Billings was scared half to death on his watch. The promise he'd broken the minute he laid eyes on Annie.

Yet despite all that, she still made it easy to push promises to the back of his mind, to forget about everything except the feel of her against him, the scent of her hair, the sight of her wide blue eyes staring back at him in the mirror. He wanted her hands on him, her sweet, full mouth kissing him all over. He wanted to see her naked in the light of day.

Joe wasn't sure which one of them led the other to the bed, but that's where he found himself, both of them naked on the warm comforter, surrounded by deep plush pillows, his skin afire and Annie whispering his name. He found himself kissing her slow and deep, drawing it out, found her above him, watching his face as they moved together, her gaze burning into him, his hands skimming over her silken skin.

And then something happened he never expected, emotions he couldn't begin to name crept in without warning, tangling with his physical need, and he was lost…caught up in a mindless twisting cloud of sensation and longing. He felt his self-control slipping, everything moving too fast…an invisible force pushing him close to the edge.

He rolled so that Annie was beneath him now. She moved with him perfectly, driving him mad with her hands and her mouth and her eyes. This time was different somehow. Explosive. Brain-boggling. A dream. The room became more and more hazy until his only focus was the friction and heat of their bodies, the sounds they made, the taste and scent of her skin. Those baffling emotions inside him.

Joe felt it the second she let go, felt the force of her climax as she clung to his shoulders and cried out. And then there was no holding back. His own release was a blazing flash fire of pleasure.

Minutes later, as he lay exhausted on top of her, his face in her hair, his thoughts scattered and lazy, three facts hit him like a triple punch to the gut. He was content. Comfortable. Happy.

Another first. Usually he only wanted up and out after being with a woman, to avoid the awkwardness that inevitably followed. But he didn't want to leave Annie. He wanted to hold her as long as she'd let him. He couldn't get close enough to her. He felt like he'd wither and die if he ever had to let her go.

Stunned by those facts, Joe rolled to one side, stared down into her face. Her eyes were half-closed and she looked drowsy and tousled and irresistible. He reached to touch her, saw that his hand trembled, pulled back.

Whoa.

This wasn't supposed to happen. Not to him. Not now. He was forty-one years old, for God's sake. He wasn't some kid with his head in the clouds, looking for something that didn't exist. The first time he'd thought he was in love, the time he'd married, that's the way it had been.

But he didn't *think* now. He *knew*.

Whoa.

This wasn't supposed to happen. Especially not with her. The after-effects of the greatest sex ever were playing games with his mind, that's all. That had to be all there was to what he felt, what he was thinking.

But nothing between him and Annie had ever been like it was supposed to be. Not from the moment she'd jumped into his cab. He was supposed to simply watch her, not protect her, especially not *want* to protect her. Yet a fierce desire to do just that swelled in him now. The thought of anything happening to her, of anyone hurting her, even himself, *especially* himself, made him want to hit the wall, tear it down.

She was supposed to be a spoiled, snooty rich socialite.

The kind of shallow woman he couldn't stomach. Instead she was caring and funny, smart and independent. Despite every effort not to, after they quit arguing and had their first real conversation, he had liked her immediately. Not just the way she looked, though he liked that a lot, but *her*. The way her mind worked. Her courage and humor. Even her insecurities and impulsiveness.

And the sex? It was supposed to be "just sex," not...

"Whoa." Joe said the word aloud this time, and sat up abruptly.

"Whoa?" Annie shifted, looked at him, blinked. Grabbing a pillow, she bunched it beneath her head.

"That was..." He swallowed and stared at the wall. "Wow."

"My sentiments exactly."

When he found the nerve to look into her eyes, Joe saw that they were a little smug. She slid her hand down his back, up to his neck. Afraid she'd see the truth if he looked at her too long, he glanced away. "How about I start a fire and we finish that picnic that never got started?"

Annie's stomach growled. "Does that answer your question?"

HARRY LANDAU pressed his palm against the phone's mouthpiece and jerked his head toward his office door. "Beat it, Lacy."

His sister gave him that wounded puppy look that always made him want to kick her.

"Didn't you hear me? I know you're dumb, but I didn't know you were deaf, too."

Her lip quivered.

"Now!" he yelled.

Lacy jumped. He could almost imagine a tail between her legs as she turned and scampered from the room.

"Close the door behind you," he called after her. "Easy. Don't slam it."

He moved his hand away from the phone's mouthpiece and talked into it. "Brady's in Pinesborough. She's with him."

"Good. That's not far from where I am. How'd you find them?"

"Never mind." Harry drummed his fingers on the desk. "How long will it take you to get there?"

"An hour, maybe less. Me and Prine will check out of the motel, then—"

"You've been sleeping?" Harry cursed, then clamped his jaw together hard. Having to rely on Willis and his idiot partner was playing hell with his blood pressure. He couldn't afford it any more than he could afford for his uncle to find out about this slipup. The doc had warned him if he didn't keep his temper in check he might bust a vein. "If you'd stayed after them, we might be drinking Bloody Marys and having a good laugh about all this right now."

"Cut us some slack, Landau. We were in the middle of a whiteout. The roads were slick as snot. Took us a good two hours just to go thirty miles."

Harry took deep breaths and counted to ten. "I don't know where they're staying, but you shouldn't have any trouble finding out. Pinesborough doesn't sound like a metropolis."

"Don't worry. We'll find them."

"Don't waste time doing it, either. I want that briefcase back. And I want you to see to it that Anne Macy and her new boyfriend have an unfortunate accident. You hear what I'm saying?"

"Loud and clear."

"Brady's not just helping her because she's got a hot little body and a pretty face. Knowing what I do now about his history, you can bet he smells a rat and the odor's a little too familiar. It won't take him long to sniff his way to the truth."

And if that happened, Harry would wish he'd been born into another family.

"OPEN WIDE." Annie popped a caviar-topped cracker into Joe's mouth and watched him chew. "Well, what do you think?"

He swallowed, licked his lips. "I prefer sardines. What can I say? Poor schmucks have poor taste." He slanted her a sly look and added, "Except in women."

They had moved the picnic to the center of the bed where it lay spread out between them.

"I feel like a sneaky sixteen-year-old girl sitting here stark naked in my aunt's house with a guy."

"You did this sort of thing a lot when you were sixteen, did you?"

"Hardly. I was a good girl. But if I'd known how fun it is being a naughty girl…" She wiggled her brows.

"You are definitely a naughty girl now. Naughty—" he leaned over and kissed her bare shoulder. "And very, very nice."

Annie giggled like a sixteen-year-old, too. A shiver skipped through her. She was nuts about him. Gaw-gaw, as her Aunt Tess would say. When he stopped questioning his desires and followed them, he did it with gusto. And after they'd made love, just for a moment, she'd seen a flicker of something in his eyes, something that startled her. She thought she recognized it, but she was too afraid to form the word, even in her mind. Too afraid to hope. Too afraid of saying the wrong thing again.

So she changed the subject.

"Speaking of naughty," she said, "What are we going to do about Harry?"

"Where's the briefcase?"

She nodded toward the closet. "In there."

He climbed off the bed and walked to the closet, then brought the briefcase back.

Annie took it when he slid it across the bed. She popped the latches and pulled out a stack of folders. When she reached the bottom of the case, her hand stilled. "What's this?" She frowned. "I didn't feel this before."

Joe leaned in to look. "What is it?"

"It feels like a lighter…behind the case's lining." She

looked closer, noticed a barely discernible small line of stitching along the edge that didn't match the rest. "Look, someone has sewn up a tear here."

Reaching over the side of the bed, Joe scooped his jeans off the floor and retrieved a pocket knife from his pocket. He pulled out a blade and ripped into the briefcase lining. "It's a computer flash drive." He held up the plastic cylinder for her to see. "Maybe this will explain why Landau's so desperate to get this case back. Does your aunt have a computer here?"

"I don't know. If she does, it's probably in the room at the end of the hallway. She used to have it set up as a sort of combination office and library."

"Let's go." Joe grabbed up his pants again.

Annie snatched them from his hand. "Not necessary. I'm the only one looking and I do love the sight of you in the buff." She wiggled her brows. "You have a very cute butt, Brady."

"And I'm going to freeze it off if I don't cover it up. It's five degrees outside."

In a Mae West voice, she said, "Honey, if you get too cold, let me know and Annie'll warm you right up."

Shaking his head as he started from the room, Joe said, "Baby, you've got the naughty thing down to a fine art."

Tess's makeshift office was really a small converted storage room with a desk in one corner and a computer on top of it.

"That's not a computer," Joe said, "That's a dinosaur."

"Aunt Tess isn't exactly high-tech."

He crossed to the desk, searched a slot for the flash drive.

"We're out of luck. It's too old a machine. It only takes floppy disks."

"Now what?" Annie asked.

"You know anyone in town with a computer we could use?"

"I don't come here often enough to know anybody. I think there's a public library, though. Pinesborough is pretty small. You think the library would have computers?"

"There's one way to find out." Joe started out of the office. "Let's get dressed. Guess I'm not as naughty as you. I draw the line at going into town in my birthday suit."

THEY DROVE ALONG a desolate road that wound through tall trees with icicles dripping from the branches, past frosted meadows where deer lifted their heads to watch them pass. Evergreens dotted color across the canvas of white and tan and tarnished silver.

Joe rounded a bend. A farmhouse, tucked cozy and warm into the rolling hillside, peeked back at them through glowing windows. He could count on one hand the number of times in his life that he'd been in the country. New York City's rapid pulse set the pace for his heartbeat. But as he drove through the serene countryside with Annie beside him, he felt the beat slowing and an unfamiliar yet welcome sense of peace seeping into his bones, weaving through him like the frozen stream that curled like a silver ribbon through the fluffy white blanket of snow alongside the road.

The village of Pinesborough looked as if it had frozen a

hundred years ago and never thawed, a Norman Rockwell painting come to life. Twinkling white, green and red Christmas lights brightened the overcast morning. Strings of them hung in the trees along the streets, trimmed the rafters of quaint old buildings, surrounded every window. Bundled up in hats and coats and gloves, a group of small boys carried round plastic sleds across a small park, their boots trailing footprints behind them.

Joe's thoughts drifted to his mom, and he wondered if the image resembled her old dream for him and his brother. He remembered the conversations he had overheard between his parents when he was a teenager. His mom pleading with his father to move to a "calmer" place, somewhere safe and wholesome where they could raise their boys. Like this town, he imagined. With a park to play in, and footprints trailing through pristine snow.

How different would his life be now if that had happened, Joe wondered? Would he have become a cop? Would he be married right now with a house full of rug rats? Spend weekends teaching them how to swing a bat or cast a fishing line? Would his brother Pete be alive with a wife and kids, too? His father a happy old granddad? His mother surrounded by family instead of only one banged-up, cynical, middle-aged son?

Annie pointed out the library, a converted redbrick three-story house. Three cars lined the curb so Joe parked across the street in front of another old house and they went inside. The library had two computers, both occupied. The librarian, a pretty young woman named Mary, her brown hair in a loose braid, told them to come back in forty-five minutes to an hour and she would reserve one for them.

"How about we grab a burger somewhere, then buy a few groceries to kill time?" Joe asked as he and Annie walked out onto the library porch. "Our picnic didn't quite do the trick."

"That sounds good." Annie stuck her hands into the pockets of the hooded down jacket she had borrowed from Tess's closet along with a pullover sweater and a faded pair of jeans. She had found clothes in the guest room for Joe, too, though she had no idea who they belonged to. One of Tess's friends, she supposed. The jeans were a little loose, but they were clean and dry.

Joe wrapped an arm around her shoulders and squeezed. "Too cold to walk?"

"No, I'd like to." They started down the steps. "It feels so festive here. With all that's been going on, I almost forgot about Christmas."

Walking alongside her, Joe couldn't recall when he'd ever felt more happy. He guessed that was crazy, to feel so good when they were in so much trouble. They had been shot at, visited by the cops, followed. Even if they got the goods on Landau, Annie might still be held liable for breaking and entering, as well as for theft. But right now, in this remote old-fashioned little town with her at his side, he felt as if nothing could touch them, as if nothing ever would.

He wished they could freeze in time, too, like the town. Stay caught in this moment forever, safe and happy, free from the outside world and all its ugliness, all the problems that awaited them there.

Annie touched his cheek, her gloves warm against his skin. "You're quiet. Is everything okay?"

Leaning down, he brushed his lips against hers. "I was just thinking how nice and peaceful it is here. I'm going to hate to go back to the city after this."

She looped her arm through his. "Me, too."

They turned at the end of the block and started toward the center of the village. As they passed the park, the group of boys pulling sleds came into view, their laughter and voices sharp and clear in the stillness of the early afternoon. Stopping to watch them sail and tumble down the hill, Joe drew crisp, clean air into his lungs then blew it out in puffs of white.

"Nice day, isn't it?" a raspy voice called.

Joe turned to see someone approaching from down the sidewalk, a scarecrow of an old man with a weathered face and a slight limp. His red hunter's hat with furry ear flaps made him look like a skinny Elmer Fudd.

"Yeah," Joe said when the old man paused beside them. "It is if you're a polar bear, I guess."

Elmer cackled, his grin crinkling his face like a prune. He rubbed his gloved hands together. "Keeps the blood pumping." He glanced at Annie, then back to Joe and winked. "I see you got yourself something better to do that, though."

Joe chuckled, and Annie said, "I'll take that as a compliment."

"You should. You should," the old man said. "That's how I meant it."

"Could you suggest a good place for lunch?" Joe asked.

"Stars Diner. I'm headed there now." He pointed toward the town square. "Happy to show you the way."

"Thanks so much," Annie said. "But I bet we can find it. I think we're going to watch these boys a few minutes longer."

The old man shifted his gaze to the sledders. "They do put a smile on your face, don't they?" His eyes twinkled. "Make me feel my years, though. I used to sled in this park when I was their age." He winked again. "Had my first kiss here, too."

They talked a minute more, then he said goodbye and limped away. Joe watched him go, thinking that he had never met anyone more full of life or so unabashedly happy.

"I wonder what it'd be like to live in a place like this?" he asked Annie when they left the park ten minutes later.

"A city boy like you?" She laughed.

"Why is that so funny?"

"I'm trying to picture you in thirty or so years in a hat with ear flaps."

Joe shrugged. "Yeah, I guess I don't exactly fit in."

"Not exactly."

"It might be a kick to give it a try, though. I think I could get used to wearing overalls and having strangers greet me on the street like we're old friends. And the quiet, I could get used to that, too. No car horns blaring, or sirens wailing, or neighbors arguing through the walls."

Her eyes narrowed. "You're serious."

"Just speculating." He pulled her closer as they walked. "How about you? Would you go crazy in a town this small?"

"I've never really thought about it." As they turned another corner onto the square, she pointed out the diner. "There's the place that sweet guy told us about." They started across the street, and Annie looked up at Joe. "What brought all this on? You aren't trying to find a place for me to hide out for the rest of my life, are you? I doubt a town like this only a few hours from the city is out of Harry's or Reno's reach."

"I'm not looking for a hideout," Joe said, but he wasn't so sure that wouldn't be a good idea.

When they reached the diner, he opened the door and motioned her through ahead of him into the warmth. Immediately, aromas of sizzling meat, coffee and fresh, yeasty bread had his mouth watering. Answering the friendly greetings of several patrons, they chose an empty booth and sat.

If Reno was also mixed up with whatever was on that flash drive, then Joe couldn't say for certain how much or how little danger Annie actually faced. He had no idea how far Landau would be willing to go to keep Annie quiet; he didn't know enough about the man's history. But he was convinced that Reno had sent someone to silence Emma

Billings last year, and that Harry's uncle wouldn't think twice about doing the same with Annie.

A cold sliver of fear sliced through his heart. This time, he wouldn't slip up. Whatever it took, he would keep Annie safe. Even if it *did* mean moving her across country. Or across the world.

ANNIE COULDN'T PIN DOWN Joe's mood. He had seemed relaxed as they drove into the village, more relaxed than she had seen him in the short time they'd spent together. Then, outside the library, those two little grooves between his brows had deepened, as they often did.

Uh-oh, she'd thought. He was about to start his "I don't want to hurt you, I'm no good for you, you're out of my league" routine again and ruin a perfect day. If that had been his intention, though, the little old man in the funny red cap had sidetracked him and returned Joe's easy smile.

Now the cloud of doom had descended again. If only she had an inkling about what was on his mind, she could decide how to deal with it and set him at ease.

Joe grabbed two menus from behind the napkin dispenser, handed Annie one then opened his. He laughed: "Get a load of this. The John Travolta Burger—No Grease," he read. "The Julia Roberts Mystic Pizza."

Annie opened her own menu and skimmed the selections. "Mel Gibson's Spicy Chili—Only For Bravehearts. Someone around here has a sense of humor."

"A cheesy one."

"Shhh," Annie warned as a waitress approached the table.

Joe estimated the woman's age to be close to his and Annie's, though she had the deeply wrinkled skin of someone who spent every spare hour outdoors. She wore jeans and a white apron over her green sweater. The star-shaped name tag pinned over her left breast read Kate.

"Welcome to Stars," Kate said. "It's good to see new faces in here." Nodding toward the next table where two elderly men sipped coffee, she added, "Of course, I like the old faces, too." She flashed the old-timers a grin, spreading fans of wrinkles at the outer corners of both bright-green eyes. "Especially these two good-looking devils."

The men hooted and cackled.

Recognizing one of them as the old man who had greeted them at the park, Annie waved at him. His hat was off, and freckles covered his shiny bald head.

The rotund man beside him slapped his knee. "Katie-girl, I love the way you sweet-talk but if you're trying to get on my good side, I'd rather have a piece of your apple pie."

Annie recognized the whistling sound the heavier man made when he spoke. She leaned toward Joe and whispered, "I think he's the guy who towed us out of the ditch."

"Aren't you supposed to be on a diet, Nate?" Kate asked the heavyset man, her eyes narrowing on him accusingly.

"He is," the skinny bald guy interjected. "He's cut down to two pieces a day instead of three."

Several people around the café chuckled and called out cajoling comments.

"You got a lot of room to talk, Coleman," Nate said. "You eat ever bit as much as me, you just got a tape worm in your gut. Can't understand why a geezer my age should diet, anyhow. Might as well enjoy what time I got left."

Coleman lifted his water glass. "I hear you, buddy."

"Now if I can only convince Sally of that," Nate said. "She's got me eating fat free and walking to nowhere every morning on that danged contraption of hers. I got to sneak over here just to keep from wasting away from starvation." Leaning back in his chair, he patted his round belly. "Guess she thinks she can keep me alive forever."

"Could be she's just hoping you can keep up with her while you're here." Coleman winked at Joe. "That's what happens. Just wait. You'll see. One day you'll putter out, but that pretty lady with you will still be buzzing along."

Nate slapped his knee and laughed, his breath escalating from a whistle to a wheeze. "Ain't that the sad truth? You may not believe it now," he said to Annie in a confidential tone, "but the time'll come when you'll have to slip a little pill in his juice every morning if you want to get a rise outta him by nightfall."

As snickers sounded around the café, Kate shook her head. "You two hush. You're going to offend these nice people."

Watching for Joe's reaction, Annie bit her lip to hold back a laugh of her own.

He leaned back in his seat, narrowing his gaze on the mischievous old twosome. "I'll let both of you in on a little secret," he said, a gleam lighting his eyes. "You've got to use it or lose it."

"Use it all you want," Nate wheezed. "But don't fool yourself, you're still gonna need that little bitty pill some day."

"I should've known better than to get you two started," Kate huffed, then returned her attention to Annie and Joe. "Sorry about them. What'll you have?"

After they placed their orders, Annie stood and started off toward the restroom.

"Good to know you two didn't get stuck again," Nate called out. "I was worried. That hot rod's not made for ice."

"She held her own," Joe answered, sounding as if the old man had insulted his mom instead of his car.

"Thanks again for pulling us out," Annie said as she passed the old men.

At a table across the way, a woman read the local paper. A wedding invitation to the entire town of Pinesborough filled the back page. Annie thought of her own wedding, the weeks she'd spent with Aunt Tawney fretting over who to put on the invitation list and who to leave off, the hundreds of expensive announcements on crème-colored stock with gold engraving that had gone to waste.

Minutes later when she left the restroom and made her way back to the table, she found Joe at the table with the old men, sitting at the edge of his chair, absorbed in a story

Coleman was telling. Joe leaned toward the other men, his forearms propped against his thighs. Coleman delivered the punch line and slapped Joe on the back with a laugh, then swiped a French fry off Nate's plate.

She paused by the counter to watch them, wondering if there was once a time when Joe had shared the same easy male-to-male rapport with his father and brother. Just for a moment she wondered, as he had, how it would be to live in a town like Pinesborough. A simple, friendly place without pretensions, where life moved slowly and people stopped to chat on the street with strangers, where brides invited the whole town to the wedding via the newspaper.

When Nate spotted Annie, the men's conversation stopped abruptly with a clearing of throats and a cough or two. She narrowed her eyes. "What are you guys talking about, anyway?"

"Just swapping war stories," Joe answered, and grinned.

She crossed her arms. "More like dirty jokes, I'm thinking."

As she started over to join them, Coleman stopped talking and gripped the table's edge. His face and bald head turned a purple-tinged shade of red. His eyes widened and his mouth fell open as he reached a trembling hand toward her.

"He's choking," Annie gasped and the hairs on her arms stood on end.

The table fell silent and Annie heard a plate clatter against the counter, then Kate's sharp sound of distress as she darted around the counter. Joe's chair squealed against the linoleum floor as he jumped up and ran behind Coleman. He slid his arms beneath the wiry man's armpits, wrapped them around his thin chest. Fisting his right hand, he placed it below the man's rib cage, flattened his left palm over the fist, squeezed in and up in one fast motion.

"Spit it out, Cole," Nate said, his voice wavering.

Coleman made a strangled sound. A tear rolled down his cheek.

Joe pushed again and a French fry shot out of Coleman's mouth, sailed across the table and landed on Nate's shoulder. Shouts and applause went up around the diner.

"That'll teach ya to keep your hands off my plate," Nate teased, relief spilling from his voice.

Annie's heart rate slowed to a more normal pace. For the first time, she noticed the group of people who had gathered around the table.

Kate grabbed a glass of water, knelt at Coleman's side and said, "You okay, Dad?" She brought the glass to his lips and he sipped then started coughing again. She glanced up at Joe. "Thank you. You probably just saved my father's life."

"Glad I could help."

"Are you two just passing through or are you in Pinesborough for a visit?"

Joe shot a quick glance at Annie and said, "We're spending one night here on our way to the ski area."

"You picked the perfect time for skiing. I hear the powder's great right now." Kate shifted her gaze between them, suspicion in her eyes. "Didn't peg you two as skiers for some reason." Turning, she started back toward the counter with the cook at her side. "By the way, your lunch is on the house." She nudged the man. "It just so happens, I sleep with the owner."

Joe patted Coleman on the back and asked if he was okay. Coleman assured him that he was, and Joe and Annie returned to their booth.

Annie propped her elbows on the table. "Well, you were certainly impressive. I think you've made some fans."

"No more than you." He wiggled his brows and nodded at the old men. "The boys like your ass."

"They do, do they?"

"They watched you all the way to the restroom." His mouth turned up at one corner. "Coleman may not chew worth a damn, but there's nothing wrong with his eyesight."

Annie laughed, relieved to be talking about something other than the trouble that had brought them here.

When Kate arrived at the table with their food a few minutes later, she said, "I'm sorry, I don't think I introduced myself. I'm Kate Kilroy." She nodded toward the grill. "That's my husband, Ray."

Ray looked over his shoulder and said, "Hey."

"Kilroy…" Annie glanced at Nate.

"Nate is Ray's dad and Coleman is mine," Kate explained.

"Wow." Annie laughed as she glanced at the two men. "The whole family's here."

"Oh, there's a lot more where they came from," Kate said with a laugh of her own. She looked from Annie to Joe and back again expectantly.

Annie said, "I'm, uh, Anne." She slid Joe a look, caught the slight narrowing of his eyes. The movie poster of Katherine Hepburn behind his head caught her attention and she added, "Anne Hepburn."

Kate looked at the poster briefly and her eyebrows rose as she met Annie's gaze and said, "Hi, Anne."

Annie lifted her glass of tea. "And this is Joe—"

"Hepburn," Joe finished smoothly. He smiled. "Anne's husband."

Kate's attention slid to Annie's left hand holding the tea glass, and Annie was acutely aware of the fact that she wasn't wearing a wedding ring. "Well then," Kate said, "Nice to meet you both."

Joe broke the awkwardness of the moment by asking Kate questions about Pinesborough.

"Shopping here leaves a lot to be desired. A woman has to drive to the next decent-sized town if she needs something to wear that's not casual. But I guess there's worse things than that. It's a good, safe place to live and raise kids."

"It's not lacking in friendly folks, that's for sure," Annie said.

Joe glanced at Nate and Coleman's table. "Or people with a sense of humor."

"I'm always happy to meet anyone who isn't too uptight to appreciate our local bad boys," Kate said with a sheepish grin. "You two have made a couple of loyal friends today in Dad and Nate. Not only for what you did, either. They love a pretty woman who'll tolerate them and any man who'll laugh at their bawdy jokes."

"Aha." Annie narrowed her eyes at Joe. "So I was right about the jokes."

"Hiding that fact from you, was he?" Kate chuckled. "As a matter of fact, I think Joe even told one of his own. He fits right in."

Annie noticed how pleased Joe looked by the woman's comment.

CHAPTER 12

Forty minutes later, not only were Annie and Joe on a first-name basis with Kate and Ray Kilroy, Coleman and Nate, they also knew the life story of Nadine Milin, manager of Food Queen Market, where they bought four bags of groceries. They knew details about Nadine's migraine headaches, the birth of her first grandbaby, the story of Pinesborough's half-senile sheriff accidentally locking himself in a jail cell overnight, and the gossip about Nadine's hairdresser and the local Presbyterian minister.

And Nadine knew quite a bit about them, as well. She had heard from Janice Ryan, a bank teller who'd been eating lunch at Stars a few minutes earlier, that a couple visiting Pinesborough had saved Coleman Gray from choking on one of his son-in-law's overdone French-fried potatoes. Anne and Joe *Hepburn* were fast becoming legends around town.

Annie laughed as they loaded the grocery sacks into the trunk of Joe's car. "After less than an hour, I feel like I know more people here than I do after living six months in New York City. And I know them *better*."

"Me, too. That worries me a little. We probably should have tried to stay incognito in case someone shows up asking about us." He closed the trunk and gestured toward the library. "Ready, Mrs. Hepburn?"

She nodded and smiled. "I can't wait to see what's on that flash drive."

Joe took her hand and they turned toward the library across the street.

Before they'd taken two steps, the door opened and a man stepped out.

"Get down!" Joe said, tugging her arm and pulling her down with him. They crouched at the back of the car, then scrambled around to the side of it to hide themselves from the library's front doors.

"What's wrong?" Annie whispered.

"Willis and Prine. They just came out of the library with the librarian. They must've spotted my car here."

"Did they see us?"

"I don't think so."

He scanned the surrounding area. The street was clear of traffic and pedestrians. The house across from Joe's car was quiet and still.

"Let's try to make it across the yard and around to the back of this house." Joe squeezed Annie's hand. "I'll be right behind you." He lifted up just high enough to see the library porch. The two cops were still talking to the young woman who had promised earlier to save them a computer. "Okay," Joe whispered. "Stay low." He let go of her hand.

Crouched down, Annie started across the yard.

Joe followed, risking another look over his shoulder at the library porch. His heart jumped when Willis started to turn in their direction.

In that instant, the librarian lifted her eyes to Annie, then shifted to Joe. Their gazes locked briefly, and the young woman turned away and touched Willis's shoulder. Joe feared she was about to point them out, and his pulse shot up to his throat. But when Willis and his partner faced the girl, the librarian glanced quickly at Joe again and something in her expression told him she meant to help them.

He didn't stop to question why a woman he and Annie had only exchanged a few brief words with earlier would come to their aid. Instead, he took advantage of the opportunity she had just given them to run.

Joe caught up to Annie, grabbed her arm, pulled her along until they made it to the backyard.

Gasping for air, she fell against the wall of the house. "That man, the one with the brown hair, he's the cop who was in Harry's office."

Joe braced his palms against his thighs and sucked in deep breaths of air. "That's Randy Willis."

He wasn't surprised by Annie's news. Now that she had recognized Willis's face as well as his voice, Joe didn't doubt that their suspicions about Willis and Landau were true.

Taking Annie's hand, he set off on a zig-zagging route toward the diner where they'd had lunch, uncertain where else to go.

They ran down snow-rutted alleyways and slippery side streets, ducking behind trees or shrubbery each time they neared the village's main street. Twice they spotted Willis and Prine, who were also on foot.

At the side of an office building across the street from Stars, Annie and Joe paused to catch their breath and wait for a safe time to cross the street. Annie barely felt the cold; she hadn't been this keyed up since Sasquatch shot at her. "How could they have tracked us here?"

"Maybe I didn't lose them when I took that exit off the highway, after all."

Annie glanced around Joe and down the street. "They're going inside the grocery store."

He took her hand again. "Let's go."

When they entered Stars, Coleman and Nate were beside the door zipping into their coats. The lunch rush had ended. Except for the two old men and Kate and Ray, the diner was empty.

Annie's chest and throat burned from exertion and drawing ice-cold air into her lungs.

"We need your help," Joe said, and closed the door. He stood to the side of the window, peering out.

Nate clasped Annie's shoulder, his worried expression reminding her of her own father. "Sit down before you fall down." He led her to a chair away from the window.

Kate came around the counter with the ever-silent Ray following close behind. "Are those cops after you? They were in here nosing around."

"Right after the two of you left," Coleman added. "Asked Katie and Ray all kinds of questions, then started on us."

Kate crossed to where Annie sat. "They had your picture." She nodded toward Joe. "And they gave a pretty good description of you." Katie crossed her arms. "Ray and I told them we never saw you before."

Ray nodded.

Nate patted Annie's hand. "I never saw you, either."

"Or me," Coleman echoed.

Relief and gratitude rushed through Annie. "Thank you." Still panting, she looked from one face to the next. "All of you."

"Yeah, thanks," Joe said, keeping his gaze on the window. "You just bought us some time."

Katie narrowed her eyes. "I'm guessing you two aren't really passing through on a ski trip."

"Sorry about that," Annie said with a wince.

Joe turned away from the window long enough to say, "My name is really Joe Brady."

Annie smiled nervously. "And I'm Anne Macy. Call me Annie."

Nate studied her for a few seconds, then said, "Well,

what do you know? I do see a resemblance to Tess. When I dug you out of that ditch this morning I figured you were just renting her place. Are you Tess's daughter?"

"I'm her niece. I'm surprised you didn't know. News seems to travel fast around here."

"Speaking of which," Joe added, "You didn't tell the librarian about us, did you?"

"Mary?" Kate chuckled. "She's my daughter. She called after you two finished your lunch and left, and Ray told her about how you saved her granddad from choking on a fry. She figured you were the same strangers who'd stopped by the library earlier to use a computer."

"Your daughter did us a big favor a few minutes ago," Joe said, then explained how Mary had diverted the two men's attention so he and Annie could escape.

"That's my Mary," Coleman said.

Joe returned his attention to the window. "They're a few blocks down and headed this way." He stepped back, let the curtain fall.

Annie's stomach turned over. No one had even asked why two policemen might be after them. No one seemed to care. But she couldn't expect them to hide a couple of fugitives. And she wouldn't blame them if they called the sheriff. Why would they want to bring trouble down on themselves by helping two strangers? They would be acting on pure instinct, blind trust.

Just as Joe had when he rescued her from Harry.

Annie looked at each of their faces. At Joe's. Suddenly,

she realized he had more in common with these small-town folks than she had ever realized.

Coleman pulled off his hat. "Answer me one question."

"Anything," Joe said.

"You two didn't murder some poor son-of-a-bitch or rob a bank, did you?"

"No, sir," Annie said. "Not anything even close to that."

The old man pursed his lips and studied them closely. "Didn't do something else bad to somebody who didn't deserve it?"

Annie thought of Harry, the way he treated his sister, the way he had tried to force himself on her at the Christmas party. "No—"

"He deserved it," Joe finished. "And what we did to him wasn't nearly bad enough. We can explain, I promise, but there's no time now." He cast a nervous glance at the window again then nodded toward a movie poster on the wall of Marlon Brando in *The Godfather*. "Those cops that are after us? They're about as honest as Don Corleone, there."

Coleman lifted a hand to silence him. "Say no more. Doesn't matter. You're right. We don't got time for explanations. Come here, Annie. I have an idea."

Annie stood and hurried to him.

Coleman gave Nate his red hat and looked Annie up and down. "You're almost my size," he said slipping out of his coat. "Take off your jacket and put this on." He gave her his coat. "Tuck your hair up under my hat."

"Hurry," Joe said, staring out the window again.

Katie twisted Annie's hair into a knot and Coleman crammed the red hat on top of her head as she zipped up the old man's coat.

"Toss me your keys, Nate," Coleman said, as if used to giving orders. "Joe and I are taking your Jeep. You walk Annie to your place." When Joe looked over his shoulder, Coleman explained, "It's closest and in the opposite direction from where those two are headed."

Nate reached into his coat pocket, pulled out a ring of keys and threw them to his friend.

Coleman nodded at the door. "Go on. And don't look back or walk too fast. Just act like nothing's out of the ordinary."

Swallowing past the lump of anxiety in her throat, Annie started for the door. As Nate reached to open it, she glanced over at Joe.

"Don't worry, young lady," Coleman said. "I'll take care of him. We'll be along soon."

In any other situation, his calling her a "young lady" and his comment about taking care of Joe would have amused her. A tired little shriveled-up man with a limp protecting an ex-cop still in his prime. An ex-cop whom she happened to know carried a gun beneath his coat. But as she looked into Coleman's pale eyes, saw the shrewd determination in them, she believed him.

Nate said, "Ready?"

Annie nodded.

Behind her, Coleman said, "Katie-girl, put Annie's coat in the storage closet. Ray…"

WEARING KATE'S HUSBAND Ray Kilroy's sunglasses, Yankees cap and heavy down coat, the collar zipped up past his chin, Joe walked out of Stars Diner with Coleman beside him. He'd had to leave his leather jacket with Kate and she hid it in back.

Joe hooked his hand under one of Coleman's arms and guided the limping older man to the Jeep parked out front. He nodded briefly at Willis and Prine, who were just steps away from the diner, paid them no more attention than he would a couple of strangers he might pass on the street, though his heart rapped against his chest like machine-gun fire.

"I don't need my son-in-law to carry me to the car," Coleman grumbled, coughing and sputtering, playing the part of grouchy, confused old man to perfection. "I choked on a French fry, not cyanide. I just don't feel like driving. All I want you to do is take me home so you can get back to work."

Joe sighed long and deep, as if completely at his wit's end. He opened the Jeep's passenger door and waited for Coleman to climb in. To his relief, Willis and Prine entered the diner after only a cursory glance their direction. Still, Joe didn't plan to relax until he and Annie were back together and tucked away safely somewhere out of sight.

Once behind the wheel, he pulled away from the curb

and turned to Coleman. "Thanks, buddy. I can't begin to tell you how much this means to Annie and me."

"My pleasure. Kind of fun, as a matter of fact. We don't get much excitement around here." The old man ducked low in the seat. "Anyhow, I owed you one."

"Where we headed?"

"Turn left at the light, then down four blocks and left again. Nate's house is third on the right." He reached overhead and pulled a garage door opener off the visor. "We'll pull into the garage in back."

The light turned red. Joe stopped and waited even though no other cars were on the road in either direction. A block down on the left, he spotted Annie and her escort, her limp a fair but passable imitation of Coleman's gait.

"Just wave and drive on," Coleman said. "No use taking chances. Like your lady friend said, things get around fast here. People have eyes in the back of their heads, and I don't think I could explain how I'm out there walking and in here at the same time." He gave a rusty chuckle. "Besides, Nate can use the exercise."

When the light changed to green, Joe turned and passed Annie and Nate by. Coleman chuckled again. "I'm the good-looking one in the red hat."

Joe took a moment to study the older man. "I'm impressed by the way you took charge back at the diner. You didn't used to be a cop, did you?"

"Nope. Fought in the Second World War, though. Nate,

too. I learned how to take orders going in, then how to give a few, too, before it was all said and done." He turned and studied Joe. "How about you? You ever a cop?"

"Yeah, I was." He cleared his throat. "Guess you're wondering why we're running."

"Did cross my mind. You said those two cops back there are a couple of rats?"

"Yes, sir. And Annie stirred up their nest."

"So you helped her out and now you're getting bit, too."

"You could say that."

"Don't blame you." Coleman gave a conspiratorial wink. "If I was younger and single, I'd face an army of rats for a sweet thing like that."

Joe slanted him a man-to-man look and Coleman laughed heartily. The old guy was perceptive. In the beginning, there'd been a limit to what Joe was willing to risk for Annie. And even that amount of risk had dollar signs attached to it. Her father's dollars.

Not anymore.

He thought of this morning, of making love to her, holding her afterward. The truth had blindsided him. Joe had tried since to rationalize his feelings. But now, with Willis at their heels and Annie's future in the balance, he couldn't pretend. He had fallen in love with her. There wasn't anything he wouldn't do to protect her.

"A man'll do crazy things for a woman. Can't hardly wait to hear what this one has you messed up in."

"It's a long story."

Coleman scooted up, peeked over the dash. "It'll wait until we're inside." He pointed at a small yellow house up ahead. "This is Nate's place. Pull to the back."

THEY STAYED at Nate's until nightfall, though Coleman went home exhausted long before. After meeting Nate's wife, Annie understood why their son Ray was so quiet. Sally Kilroy was a tiny fluttering woman with a tireless tongue. Any kid growing up in her house wouldn't get a word in edgewise.

Late in the day, Sally went to the market to replace the groceries Joe and Annie had left in the trunk of the GTO. They would be driving Sally's old worn-out Buick back to Tess's place. They didn't think it would be safe to return to Joe's car to get the groceries.

While Sally shopped, Nate logged onto his new Dell computer, then pushed out of the chair, offered it to Joe and left the room.

Joe turned to Annie. "You do it. You went to a lot of trouble and risk for this."

Annie sat and slipped the flash drive into the proper slot. She glanced up at Joe, her fingers poised atop the keyboard. "For all I know, this might turn out to be nothing more than an address book or something else that won't do us any good."

He shrugged. "Let's take a look and see."

Annie returned her attention to the computer and pulled

up the directory. A list of files labeled by date flashed onto the wide blue screen. She glanced at Joe again, then clicked on the top date of more than a year earlier. After scanning the first two paragraphs of text that pulled up, she scrolled down to read more. "It's a sort of diary. Oh…read this. Look who he mentions."

"Merry Christmas to us," Joe murmured, reading over her shoulder, both of them silent as Annie scrolled through the rest of that page then the next. "What do you know…." He exhaled slowly. "I was right about Willis. He *was* skimming dope and money from busts."

"Why would Harry document this?"

"Maybe to make sure his ass was covered in case they got caught. With detailed records and names, he might've thought he could trade information for a lighter sentence."

Annie closed the first file then clicked onto the next. The entry was much like the previous one, with dates of deals, amounts exchanged and names of certain people involved.

Joe braced a hand on the desk alongside the keyboard. "You were right on about your boss, Sweet Tea. Willis transferred the dope to Landau, then Landau sold it to his customers and laundered the money through the restaurant."

"What do you think Willis got out of it?"

"Part of the profit. Landau probably disguised Willis's cut as a payment for services rendered of some sort."

"But I didn't find anything suspicious when I went through the files."

"There are a dozen ways to get around it if you know what you're doing. Maybe someone in Willis's family or a friend was in on the deal. The payments could've been made to them under the guise of a business transaction."

She nodded. "That would be easy enough. Especially if they own a food-service business." Annie leaned back in the chair. "When we get back to Tess's I'll look at the records again. Maybe now that I have a better idea of what to look for, I'll find it."

Joe gestured toward the screen. "Let's see the next file and find out what else Harry has to say."

The chair Annie sat in was oversized to accommodate Nate's large frame. She scooted to one side and patted the seat. "If you don't mind close quarters, I'll share."

"I think I can handle squeezing up close to you." He sat slightly sideways, settling his arm around her waist.

Annie brought up the next entry, then read the first few sentences aloud. "Do I understand this? Does it mean Willis wasn't only getting the drugs from raids, he was—"

Joe sat forward abruptly. "He *did* set me up."

"I'm not sure I understand."

"Willis checked out two kilos of coke that had been booked into property division after a raid. To take the kilos to court as evidence, supposedly. But the dope never made it back."

"It went to Harry. I see that, but wouldn't someone have become suspicious when Willis didn't replace it?"

"He replaced it, all right." Joe met her gaze. "With flour. The kind grandmothers use to bake cakes."

"And nobody caught on?"

"Yeah, eventually. Shortly before that happened, I'd figured out that some of what we'd confiscated was missing. I was looking into it when everything fell apart. As stupid and cocky as Willis is, he knew better than to sign his own name when he checked out the dope from property division. He falsified police documents so that another officer would be blamed."

The truth slammed into her. "He signed your name."

"Only I didn't know it was Willis. I could never figure out who would do that to me." Traces of the betrayal he'd felt flickered in Joe's eyes. "An inquiry was held, but nothing came of it. The signature didn't match mine, and nobody in property division could verify anything. But it didn't matter. The seed of doubt about me had already been planted in a lot of minds. Especially since it came on the heels of what happened with Emma Billings."

Annie touched his arm and nodded at the computer screen. "You can clear your name now."

He smiled. "Thanks to you."

Annie smiled back, then looked at the screen again. "I don't see anything here about Reno. He's the one I wanted most of all." Over the past couple of days, she'd come to terms with the fact that she might never know all the facts surrounding that final year of her mother's life, how much

Lydia had known about Reno's business dealings, if she was having an affair with him. But the bottom line was that Lydia had been her mother. Annie knew that she not only had to stop making excuses for her mom's failings, she also had to forgive her and move on, remember the good things, as Joe had advised.

But Lydia had paid with her life for whatever sins she'd committed. Annie thought it only fair that Reno paid for his sins, too.

"I doubt we'll find anything here to finger Reno. He's probably the one person Landau's too afraid of to name." Joe yawned. "I have a feeling if we stayed up all night and read through the rest of these files, we'd find other names. But I'm beat. We'll save the rest for tomorrow. After what we've already seen, I'm satisfied we at least have enough to nail Landau and Willis to the wall. Mark my words, when that happens at least one of them will trade information on Reno for a few less years in the slammer."

"We should make a copy of this while we're here," Annie said. "For backup. Just in case."

"Good idea." Joe reached for a box of blank disks on Nate's desk shelf.

CHAPTER 13

After a fitful sleep, Joe awoke just after dawn. So as not to disturb Annie, he lay very still, staring at the ceiling while his sight adjusted to the darkness. Last night, they had hid a copy of the flash drive in the glove compartment of Sally Kilroy's car. Joe thought about the information on it and was bombarded with hurtful memories of the old accusations against him, the inquiry. Now he knew the source of that particular piece of trouble. Willis had tried to ruin him. And he'd come close to succeeding.

They had never been close by any stretch of the imagination. He and Willis had never hung out together, swapped jokes or commiserated over lousy hours and even worse pay. Still, they were cops, members of the same professional family. Joe had always respected the men and women that made up that family.

He drew Annie closer and buried his face in her hair. Her warmth seeped into every fiber of his body, spreading desire and remorse in equal parts through his veins. Maybe he wasn't much better than Willis. In the beginning, he could justify Milford Macy's demand that they keep Annie unaware of his true role. But in the beginning, Joe didn't know and respect her. In the beginning, he didn't love her.

Now no good explanations existed for his continued silence. None had for more than a day. Not since that moment in the back seat of his car when Annie had offered herself to him, and he'd accepted.

As Joe slipped from the bed, he noticed that the telephone on the nightstand was off the hook. Last night, he had been teasing her about something and she'd tossed a pillow at him, knocking the receiver from its cradle. They had never replaced it. Joe put it back now before crossing the room to make a fire.

He took wood from the stack by the fireplace, a match from the mantel above it. Placing the logs onto the grate, he struck a flame and turned on the gas. The wood caught. The flames crackled. Joe returned to bed.

"That's nice," Annie murmured as he slipped beneath the covers beside her again.

He had hoped she would continue to sleep so that he could think of the best way to tell her the truth about himself. "What's nice? The fire?"

"And you." She looked up at him with a sleepy smile.

The firelight cast a honeyed glow across her skin and made her eyes sparkle, her pale hair shine. It would've been so simple to put off the truth a while longer, to keep pretending. But he couldn't do it anymore. He wouldn't.

Joe stared down at her, so beautiful in the flickering light, so trusting, so important to him. More important than he'd thought any woman ever would be. He touched her hair, pushed it away from her face.

"Is something wrong?" she whispered, her smile slowly fading.

"No."

"*Something's* bothering you."

"I'm in love with you, Annie."

She brushed her fingers across his cheek, his mouth, her gaze never leaving his. "I'm in love with you, too. I keep telling myself that's crazy considering we've known each other two days."

"I don't care if it's only been two minutes," Joe said. "We've shared more and been through more together than a lot of couples do in a lifetime. I love you."

"And that scares you?"

"It scares the hell out of me. If I lose you—"

"Why would you think that? If it's those files I took that worry you…now that we know about Harry, about Willis… now that we have proof, nobody will blame me for doing what I did."

He swallowed, looked away, then back at her. "What scares me the most doesn't have anything to do with you stealing those files. There's something I have to tell you. Annie, I—" A noise downstairs interrupted him. Joe shoved the covers aside. "Did you hear that?"

Frowning, Annie pushed up onto her elbows. "I didn't hear anything. What did it sound like?"

"Some kind of movement downstairs."

"It was probably just the wind rattling the windows."

"Maybe." Joe started to lean back again when a sharp shattering sound broke the silence. He jumped up, pulled on his jeans, grabbed his gun from the nightstand and started for the door. "Stay here," he whispered over his shoulder.

The hallway was dark, the floor cool beneath his bare feet. Joe held the snub-nosed at ready, kept his steps slow, his back to the wall as he moved toward the staircase. Gray morning light sifted up from the wall of windows in the great room below. He took a deep breath then started down, one step at a time, scanning the lower room for any movement.

At the bottom of the stairs, Joe stopped to take inventory and didn't see anything out of place. The front door was closed. He moved to the sofa, around it, taking in everything at once. The space beneath the coffee table, each shadowed empty corner, the distance to the swinging door that led to the kitchen.

A dim shaft of light speared out from beneath that door. Joe halted, drew in a long breath, let it out slowly. In three quick strides, he reached the door, pushed through it, shouted, "Freeze!"

A man with wavy silver hair who looked to be in his late sixties to early seventies stooped in front of the open refrigerator in front of an orange juice puddle and a broken glass. He blinked up at Joe with wide, startled eyes.

Joe wondered what self-respecting burglar took time to drink a glass of juice before heisting the jewels and electronics?

The man slowly stood, lifting his arms overhead while still holding a piece of glass in one hand.

Joe noticed the way his sweater and slacks hung on his tall, toned body, his expensive-looking leather shoes, the Rolex watch on his wrist. The guy didn't look like a thief. He looked like a distinguished gentleman, a mature male model in a Bloomingdale's ad.

And he looked vaguely familiar.

Keeping the gun leveled between the man's patrician eyebrows, Joe snapped, "Who are you?"

"I'm just going to set this glass down," the older man said, his words slow and precise as he lowered his hand. "Don't shoot me."

"I asked you a question."

Before he could respond, the door behind Joe burst open and Annie shrieked, "Daddy!"

Daddy? Joe glanced back at her.

She switched on the overhead light.

Milford Macy closed the refrigerator door and stepped around the puddle. "I got here as soon as I could, Annie. Thank God you're okay." He opened his arms and Annie walked over and hugged him.

Tension fell from Joe's body like slats in a lowering window blind. No wonder the guy had looked familiar. Annie resembled her father.

His client.

A new sort of tension rose up in him again. He stuffed his gun into the waistband of his jeans.

Annie stepped away from her father and turned around. "Daddy, this is Joe Brady. The man I told you about. Joe, my father, Milford Macy."

They shook hands. "Excuse my language, sir," Joe said, "But you scared the hell out of me."

Macy chuckled. "Sorry about that. I tried to call earlier after landing at the airstrip, but the line was busy."

Joe thought of the phone by the bedside and remembered replacing the receiver just minutes ago.

"Fortunately, another gentleman was out there when I landed. He drove me as far as town and dropped me at a café. A couple of men were drinking coffee there, and I hired them to drive me out here." He chuckled. "I say I hired them, the driver flew right off the handle when I tried to pay him. Funny old codger. Whistled when he talked."

"Nate," Joe and Annie said in unison.

Annie moved up beside Joe. "What are you doing here, Daddy? You know I don't like you to fly alone. Especially in weather like this."

"The storm is past. The plane was the fastest way for me to get here." He paused, his gaze shifting from Joe's bare chest to Annie's silky robe then up to her eyes. "I came to take you home."

"You wasted fuel," Annie said, and reached for Joe's hand as if for moral support. "I'm not going back to Georgia with you."

Joe met Macy's stare, watched his eyes narrow, the tips of his ears turn red. *Uh-oh.*

"You're wrong," Macy said to Annie, though his gaze remained on Joe. "I should've come sooner. My daughter wasn't part of our deal, Brady."

Joe's heart dropped like an anchor as he quickly turned to face Annie.

"Deal?" She looked back and forth between the two men.

"I can explain," Joe said, his stomach twisting into a knot. "Mr. Macy, could you give me a few minutes alone with Annie before we discuss that? I haven't had a chance to—"

"Discuss what?" Annie's fingers were so cold they shot goose bumps up his arms. She blinked at him. "Joe?"

"I was about to tell you when he showed up. Annie...I'm a private investigator. I—"

"I hired you to watch out for my daughter," Macy interrupted, "to bring her home safely, *not* to take advantage of her."

The color drained from Annie's face. She released Joe's hand and stepped back, her look of betrayal like a knife in his side.

"I can explain," Joe repeated, reaching for her.

But Annie was through the door before he could speak another word.

ANNIE DARTED UP THE STAIRS, her vision blurred by tears. She heard Joe call her name, heard her father call out to her, too, but she didn't stop. She had to get away from them. Away from the truth.

The events of the past two days flew back at her. How could she have been so gullible? So stupid? She hadn't met Joe by chance. He hadn't helped her out of the goodness of his heart. Helping her had been his *job*. He was her father's hired watchdog. They had a *deal*.

Her father had misled her about Joe, just as he had misled her about her own mother.

Even worse, *Joe* had misled her. Tricked her. He was the lowest of the low. He'd *slept* with her. Told her he *loved* her. Why? To win her trust? Keep her with him until he could deliver her safely to her father and collect his paycheck? He was no different than Lance or the others. Joe didn't want her, he was after her father's money.

At the top of the stairs, Annie headed for the bedroom. Once inside, she slammed the door behind her and twisted the lock. She leaned against the closed door.

"Annie." Joe rattled the knob. "Annie, please let me in."

"Go away." At that moment, she wasn't sure who she hated more, Joe or her father. They had plotted and schemed, and she had made it easy for them by deceiving herself, by believing what they wanted her to believe.

The past was repeating itself.

Hadn't she done that before? Convinced herself that the picture her father painted of her mother was true? That she'd been an angel, a perfect paragon of womanhood Annie should strive to be like? But it turned out her mother had only been human. As Annie was. Prone to mistakes. Easily manipulated and tricked into foolishness.

"Annie," Joe said, again, his voice low, only inches from her ear. "I made a mistake. Please let me in so we can talk."

She closed her eyes, covered her mouth with her hand. A mistake. All of it. The time they'd spent together, the words he'd spoken. Yes, she'd fallen in love with him, but hadn't she told him she didn't expect anything?

The lies, though…some of them outright, others by omission… Never confessing about his deal with her father, his job, even after they slept together. The reasons he'd given her for being at the right place when she ran out of Landau's. His declaration of love.

"Annie." It was her father's voice now on the other side of the door, and he used the same coaxing tone she remembered him using when she was a little girl and he wanted to convince her he knew best. "I never meant for you to find out this way. I didn't plan to tell you at all because I knew you wouldn't understand. But when I saw the two of you together…" His voice sharpened. "If I had known that

Brady would stoop to such low methods of winning your trust, I would have never hired him."

"I wasn't stooping…" Joe exhaled noisily. "That isn't what I was doing." He sounded miserable.

"Try to see it from my perspective, Annie," her father continued. "You ran off to New York City just like your mother did. I knew you were angry with me. Then you got a job as a waitress. It didn't make sense. With your work experience, why would you want to wait tables? That's when I started to worry that you were up to something that could get you into trouble with the same people your mother—" His voice faltered. "Reno was in the restaurant business. So can you blame me for checking up on your boss to see if there was any connection?"

"Are you ever going to get it through your head that I'm a grown woman? I don't need or want you to check people out for me."

"Your mother was a grown woman, too."

"I'm not my mother."

"I was beside myself, afraid you were in over your head."

"So you hired a cab driver to protect me? Or is that a lie, too, Joe? A cover…"

"No, I've driven a cab part-time since I quit the force while—"

"You lied to me, Daddy. You lied so that I'd do whatever you wanted instead of letting me make my own decisions. You trusted a stranger's judgment over mine."

"Mr. Brady is also a private detective."

"So I hear."

"He was recommended by Ed Simms, a retired investigator who checked out Frank Reno for me after your mother's death."

"*I* didn't lie to you," Joe said. "Not about anything important."

"And what about what you said this morning, Joe? Was that important?"

"Of course it was," he said quietly. "That was the most important thing of all."

For several moments, only silence emanated from the other side of the door.

Finally, Joe said, "When your dad told Ed he needed to hire a private investigator in New York City and Landau's name came up, Ed's radar kicked in. He's an old family friend…used to be a cop with my dad. We talk about things. He knew why I'd turned in my badge and that I was trying to piece together all that had happened to me."

"So what you're saying is that you just didn't tell me everything, is that it, Joe? You didn't exactly lie, you simply left out a few crucial details. You have some nerve to think that you can pick and choose the information you think I need to know. Both of you."

"I'm telling you everything now. Ed knows the connection between Landau and Frank Reno. So when your father mentioned him, Ed called me." He paused. "Look, I didn't want to take this case. Even before I met you, I didn't like the fact that your father was keeping so much from you and expecting me to follow suit."

"Mr. Brady," her father hissed.

"It's the truth. I didn't like it one damn bit. But I felt I had to take the case anyway. I couldn't pass up the chance to see if it might lead me a step closer to nabbing Reno. And, the fact is, I needed the cash."

Annie pushed away from the door. She needed to think, and she couldn't as long as they were hovering over her. "Go away. Both of you. I'm going to take a shower."

She walked to the bathroom, turned on the shower and stared into the spray, too stunned to take off her robe and get in, too numb with shock to cry or even scream from frustration. She thought of her mother, of the betrayal and humiliation and self-recrimination she must've felt the moment she realized she had trusted the wrong man, that Frank Reno had taken advantage of her.

Annie closed her eyes and whispered, "Mama." Now she understood how easy it was to make a mistake, to trade your pride for a dream, something that didn't really exist, that had never existed.

A squeak pricked through her hazy state of mind. Opening her eyes, Annie turned toward the sound.

Willis stood in the bathroom doorway.

Before she could scream, he lunged and grabbed her, covered her mouth with his hand, pinched her nostrils together so she couldn't breathe. He shoved her head under the streaming hot water and held it there.

"The briefcase." Yanking her head from beneath the spray, he allowed her one quick breath. "Tell me where the briefcase is."

JOE HAD TO BITE his lip to keep from calling Milford Macy every foul name he knew as he followed him down the stairs, through the great room and into the kitchen.

"What in the hell were you thinking?" he snapped. "That was no way to tell her. You knew how she'd react."

Macy went to the window and opened the shutters. "It slipped out when I realized what you've been up to," Macy said angrily. He paused to glare at Joe. "I should rearrange your face, you sorry good-for-nothing son of a bitch."

Joe held Macy's gaze without flinching. "I deserve that. But don't fool yourself. You're no innocent in all this, either. You might have meant well, but you're just as guilty of humiliating Annie as I am."

Macy's face flushed. He lifted his chin. "I would never intentionally hurt my daughter. I happen to love her."

Joe crossed his arms, rubbed his hands up and down them, cold all the sudden. "So do I."

"You barely know her."

"I know her better after only a few days than you do after a lifetime. Have you ever talked to her as an adult rather than as a child? If not, you're about twenty years late getting started. It's—" Joe stopped talking abruptly and followed Macy's worried glance toward the swinging door they'd just come through. "What's wrong?"

"I hear something."

Turning, Joe pushed through the door again and entered the great room. The door leading onto the porch stood ajar, creaking quietly as the wind blew against it. How had he missed that before?

But he knew how. He'd been so upset with Macy, he couldn't see anything else but the red flare of his own anger. He'd let himself become distracted. Again.

"No wonder it's so cold in here," Macy said from behind him. "I would've sworn I closed that when I came in."

The hair on the back of Joe's neck prickled as he recalled checking the door when he came down this morning. "You did." Pulling his gun from his waistband, he bolted toward the stairway. This couldn't be happening. Not to Annie. He couldn't have let someone slip past him again like he did the night he guarded Emma Billings.

Joe took the stairs two at a time, and when he reached the bedroom door, he heard the shower running. He tried the knob, found it still locked. "Annie!" he called, and she cried out. Aiming his gun at the lock, Joe fired and pushed through the door.

On her knees beside the dresser, Annie struggled to catch her breath. Water dripped from her robe and hair onto the floor.

Willis stood over her, aiming a gun at her head, a gasoline can and Landau's briefcase at his feet. "Back off, Brady."

Lifting his hands out in front of him, Joe stepped backward. From behind, he heard Annie's father gasp her name.

"You too, Slick," Willis said to Macy, then nodded at the gun Joe held. "Drop it on the floor."

Joe lowered the gun.

"Toss it over here close to me. Nice and easy." When the gun hit the floor, Willis kept aim on Annie and stooped to retrieve it, then wedged it into his belt. "Now…where are the copies you made of these files?" Willis nudged Annie's temple with the gun barrel.

Keeping his hands out in front of him, Joe said, "We didn't make copies. There wasn't time."

"I saw your car at the library. I figure you were there to make copies. I tore that GTO apart and didn't find anything, so they're here somewhere." He shrugged. "If you won't tell me where, guess I'll just have to play it safe and torch the place."

"No! Don't burn down my aunt's house!" Annie cried out. "There aren't any copies in—"

Willis jerked her to her feet, pressed the revolver into her side and nodded toward Joe. "Brady, you take a walk to the bed and get comfortable." He shifted to Annie's father. "Slick, turn around and back toward me with your hands up. Slowly."

Joe glanced at Milford Macy, saw terror in his eyes. Willis

planned to toast them along with the house, and the old man knew it. Macy reached Willis at the same time Joe reached the bed. Joe's heart slammed against his chest and Annie screamed when Willis shifted the gun and hit the back of Macy's head. Annie's father passed out cold and crumpled to the floor.

Annie spun around and started pummeling Willis with her fists. He caught her around the waist and pulled a pair of handcuffs from beneath the back of his coat. "Miss Macy is going to help me out here," he said.

She shook her head and struggled against him. "No. You'll have to do it yourself."

Joe had never felt more helpless, more frustrated and angry as he watched the tears spill down her cheeks. "Why did you get involved with Frank Reno, Willis?" he asked, trying to buy time. "He's the one running this show, isn't he?"

"What do you think?"

"I don't think, I know."

"Took you long enough to figure it out."

"You were a good cop. One of the best."

"And where did that get me? I've made more money in the past year working on the side than I'll earn in five as a cop."

"Do you really think you can get away with this? I've talked to some people. They'll link this to you soon enough."

Willis chuckled and shook his head. "Sometimes you can be a real dumb-ass, Brady. That's why you made the perfect stool pigeon. *They* aren't coming after me or anybody else involved in this. We've covered our tracks."

Joe suddenly wondered who else was named in Landau's diary, and wished desperately he'd taken the time to read it to the end.

CHAPTER 14

"Did you hear what I said? Cuff Brady to the bed."

Annie glanced down at the handcuffs, then up at Willis. "And I said do it yourself." She dropped the cuffs to the floor.

He bent, snatched the cuffs up, dragged her over to the bed, then pointed the gun toward where her father lay unconscious.

"No! Don't shoot him!" She darted a desperate glance from her father to Joe. She didn't care about nailing Reno or Harry anymore. She only wanted the two men she loved most to live. *She* wanted to live. "The copy—" She looked up at Willis. "It's on a disk. There's a car in the garage, an old Buick. The disk is in the glove compartment."

"Good girl." His lip curled up. "I'll make sure the car burns, too. Now *cuff* him."

She twisted, tried to jerk her arm from his grasp. "I told you what you wanted—you can't do this!"

He pushed her hard against the bed. "Watch me."

"Leave her alone!" Joe sat up abruptly, but eased back again when Willis cocked the trigger.

Trembling, Annie bent over Joe. Her fingers brushed his arm, and she fought back more tears. "I'm sorry," she whispered, then forced herself to meet his gaze.

She saw love in his eyes. Joe loved her. She was sure of it. He hadn't lied about that. In that instant, Annie forgave him. And she forgave her father. The past was over. The only thing that mattered now was finding a way out of this mess, a miracle that would allow them all a future.

When Joe was handcuffed to the headboard, Willis tugged Annie backward to where the briefcase sat. He shoved her to her knees, made her pop the latches and open the lid. Stepping to her side, he reached for the gasoline can.

Fumes filled the room as he doused the contents. She turned away, heard the scratch of a match, smelled the pungent scent of sulfur, saw flames leap in her peripheral vision as the files caught fire.

"Close your eyes," Willis ordered, moving next to her again and pressing the gun to her temple. "See, I'm not heartless. I'll shoot you first so you won't have to see me shoot the old man."

A terrible sense of hopelessness gripped Annie. Is this how her mother had felt that night with Frank Reno in his car? Had she given up?

Jolted by that question, Annie knew at once that she couldn't just close her eyes and passively let Willis have his way. He might kill them, but if he did, he would walk away with at least a few injuries of his own. What did she have to lose?

Annie turned her head and sank her teeth into Willis's leg. He shrieked and recoiled.

She fell to her side and rolled away from the fire.

She glanced back at Willis as a white object the size of a small cantaloupe sailed into the room and hit him in the head, exploding a spray of liquid that drenched the cowering cop and splattered Annie, as well. Willis stumbled backward as Coleman, wearing his red Elmer Fudd hat, rushed in as fast as his bad leg would carry him. He drew back his arm, threw another plump, pale cylinder at Willis, then another. Willis reeled backward, and in the next second, all two hundred and sixty or so pounds of Nate barreled through the door and into Willis, knocking him to the floor. "The key to the cuffs," he yelled at Coleman. "He put them in his pocket. I'll hold him down."

As Coleman dropped to his knees beside the two men, Annie pushed to her feet, ran over to the fire and began stamping it out.

COLEMAN CHUCKLED. "Found a bunch of those little square packets on the floor downstairs. Make pretty decent water balloons in a pinch."

Joe tried to suppress his grin but failed. He watched Annie's face turn as crimson as the tips of her father's ears at the mention of the condoms Coleman had used as a weapon to distract Willis.

"They must've fallen out of my purse," she said quietly.

He held her gaze. "That seems to happen a lot."

"The latch is bad." She glanced away.

After all that had happened, Joe had hoped she might forgive him. Or at least give him a chance to explain. But now he wasn't so sure. Awkwardness, as thick as the smoke in the air, hung between them.

Taking the handcuffs with him, Joe crossed to where Nate stood over Willis beside the smoldering briefcase. Ignoring the man's dazed protests and strangled coughs, he knelt beside him, twisted Willis's arms behind his back and clicked the cuffs into place.

"I'll call the sheriff," Nate said, and crossed to the phone.

"There's another rat in the cellar out back," Coleman said.

Joe frowned and looked up at him. "A rat?"

"His partner," Coleman explained. "After we dropped Mr. Macy off here, Nate and me were driving down the road and I spotted the guy in my mirror sneaking around the house. We knocked him out. Then we dragged him to the cellar, locked him up, and came looking for you."

Nate hung up the phone and said, "Sheriff's on his way. May take him a while to get out here. He's older than the devil. Hell, he's even older than Coleman and me. Should have retired ten years ago but nobody else in the county wants the job. Not enough action." He grinned. "Until you two showed up, anyway."

Joe tugged Willis to his feet and shoved him out the doorway and down the hall toward the stairs.

He doubted Harry Landau had filed any formal complaints with the police about Annie taking his files. Still, Joe worried about the sheriff getting involved in all this. Things were coming to a head. He guessed they'd find out soon enough if Annie would suffer any consequences for her actions.

Less than ten minutes later, Joe heard a siren's wail. He looked across the great room and caught Annie's gaze. This time, she didn't look away, allowing him to see a hint of the pain he had caused her.

Wearing her father's coat over her robe, she said, "I'm going up to throw on some clothes before the sheriff arrives." She started for the stairs.

Joe wanted to follow her, to take her in his arms and make things right. But he knew that wasn't an option. Not anymore. Now that she knew the truth about him, he wondered if he would ever hold Annie again.

TWO HOURS LATER, Annie stepped into the shower again, hoping for no interruptions this time. Earlier, she and the others had followed the sheriff into town when he took Willis and Prine to book them into the county jail. They had spent more than an hour answering questions. Annie had half expected the sheriff to detain her, and though he didn't, she knew the time might come when she'd face more questions about taking Harry's files. After all she'd been through today, the possibility that she might get in trouble for her "crime" didn't scare her. She was convinced she could survive anything, now.

Annie felt the tears coming as she thought again of her mother. For some reason, she couldn't *stop* thinking about her today. She still didn't have all the answers she'd hoped for. Maybe she never would, but she felt she at least understood her mother better now. And herself. They were alike in some ways, different in others. They had each made mistakes.

But Annie was a survivor.

As the water washed over her face, she let her thoughts drift to Joe. Falling in love with him had been almost as impulsive, passionate and reckless as anything her mother had done. But despite his deception, she couldn't regret their time together. It was through him that she had learned the most about herself. She knew her own mind, now. Who she was and who she was not. What she wanted and what she didn't.

When she had thought they were all going to die, the secrets he'd kept from her hadn't seemed important anymore. Their love was all that mattered. And that's what she had seen in Joe's eyes before Coleman and Nate arrived to save the day. Love. The best actor in the world could not pretend that look. Seeing it, Annie had forgiven him. She still did. But the hurt remained, and it would take time to forget.

Annie rinsed the suds from her hair, turned off the water. She stepped from the shower and towel-dried her hair. Then she dressed in a pair of her aunt's jeans, a T-shirt and socks.

She stretched out on the unmade bed. No matter what

happened now with Joe, she could never go back to the way things had been before she moved to New York. She was no longer the same woman, afraid to go after what she wanted, afraid to admit that the mother she remembered had often been troubled and distant, restless and selfish. Afraid her discontent with her own life might mean that people were right when they said she was like Lydia Macy.

Annie refused to make the same mistakes Lydia had. She would rely on her good sense to guide her from now on. Not her father. Not her fears. Not her emotions. And right now, her good sense told her she had to put the past in the past and move on.

Yawning, Annie let her eyes drift shut. She was exhausted. Or maybe she was only using fatigue as an excuse to postpone the inevitable conversations that lay ahead with her father and Joe. Either way, she told herself she needed to lie here for just a little while, close her eyes for only a minute.

Two hours later, Annie awoke. The room was cold. She slipped on a pair of her aunt's bulky house slippers and walked downstairs. At the bottom of the staircase, she looked out the window. Joe's GTO wasn't in the drive. She walked over to look outside.

"He's gone back to the city," her father said, coming up behind her.

Annie's heart sank. "When?"

"A couple of hours ago. Not long after you went upstairs."

Annie swallowed hard, determined not to give in to the tears she felt gathering. She hadn't wanted him to leave. She had only wanted some time alone to think before they talked. Why hadn't he at least said goodbye?

"I wrote him a check and he—"

"He took money from you?"

The look on his face was the only answer she needed. Lance's betrayal had felt like a pinprick compared to the pain that sliced through her now. She walked outside into the snow-packed driveway, away from her father's concerned gaze. Glad for the biting cold and the small measure of numbness it brought, Annie put her hands to her face and started to cry.

The door squeaked behind her and moments later she felt her father's hands on her shoulders. "You love him."

Annie couldn't face him, much less respond.

"He tore up the check, Annie."

She twisted to look at him. "What?"

"Brady tore the check in half." He held out an envelope. "He asked me to give you this."

As her father went back in the house, she pulled a folded sheet of paper from the envelope, opened it, read.

Annie, I figured you could probably use some time to yourself. I'm sorry for everything I did that hurt you. I love you. That's the truth. When you're ready to talk, you know where to find me. Joe.

Snow crunched beneath her feet as Annie started for the house. She found her father in the kitchen making a sandwich. He looked up, lowered the knife he'd been using. "I owe you an apology, Annie. I've been a fool, trying to hold onto you. I've been so afraid I'd lose you like—" He bowed his head.

"You'll never lose me." She moved toward him, placed a hand on his shoulder, noticed for the first time how old he looked, how tired. "I may be like her in some ways, but not in the ways that worry you."

"I know that, sweetheart." They went to the table, sat next to each other. "You aren't troubled like she was. I knew your mother was unhappy," he said with sadness. "I didn't want to believe it, though, so I pretended. I tried to hold onto her. I guess I held too tightly. I smothered her…that's what she said."

The anguish in his voice broke Annie's heart.

"When she died," he continued, "I did the same thing to you. You'd think I would've learned my lesson." He huffed a humorless laugh. "I was so afraid you would leave me, too. That you'd get hurt like she did. And then, when you ran to New York—"

"I'm not running away from anything, like she was. I'm running *toward* something. But wherever I end up, my life's always going to include you, don't you know that?" Annie's throat tightened. She took his hand, squeezed it. "I need you. No matter how old I get, I always will. I've tried hard to make up for her loss, but I can't anymore. I have to do what's best for me."

Her father looked across at her, his eyes shining with unshed tears. "I'm so sorry. I should've told you everything a long time ago."

"I understand now why you didn't." She blinked at him, wanting it all out, all the hurts and confusion, so that they could move past them. "What I don't understand is why you don't think I'm capable of controlling the bank?"

He frowned. "Why do you think that?"

"Matchmaking me with Lance? And before him, Avery and Chuck?"

"That had nothing to do with the bank. I wanted you to have someone. I could see you weren't content. I thought—"

"But they all three worked for you."

"I thought they were good matches. And good men." Her father scowled and shook his head. "I couldn't have been more wrong about Lance. I suppose two out of three picks isn't bad." He sent her a self-deprecating smile.

"But Aunt Tawney said—"

"Tawney?" His scowl returned. "Did she put that idea in your head? She's been assuming things and speaking for me since we were kids." He leaned over and hugged her, sat back. "I believe in learning a business from the ground up, no matter who you are. But you're ready, Annie. And I'm ready to slow down a little and let you take over some—"

"I don't want that anymore," Annie interrupted.

Her father watched her for a moment, then asked, "Does your change of heart have something to do with Brady? Honey…" He cleared his throat. "I'm not sure Joe Brady is someone you should—"

"Daddy." Annie scowled at him.

"I was just going to say," he quickly interjected, "that when I found out you'd taken off on the road together, I was worried. I never meant for anything like that to happen when I hired him. So I called the chief of police in New York City and after I explained the situation, he said Brady became something of a loose cannon toward the end of his time on the force. There are a lot of unanswered questions surrounding him. His negligence might've caused a woman he was supposed to be guarding—"

"Joe told me all about that."

"He did?"

"There was an inquiry and Joe wasn't found guilty of anything." Annie stood and began pacing the kitchen, thinking about her father's call to the police chief. "You didn't happen to mention to the chief where Joe and I were headed, did you?"

"I might've. Why?" Suddenly, his face fell. "You don't think…?"

Annie went cold. Could someone else at the station have listened in on the conversation? Or might the chief have unknowingly mentioned it to someone? The chief might've even been working with Harry. Any of those possibilities would explain how Willis and Prine had known where to find them. Someone within the police force ranks had told them. And if that were true, it meant others in the department were involved with Harry Landau and Frank Reno, as well.

The phone rang. Her father quickly rose to answer it.

Annie listened to him tell the caller that Joe was headed back to the city. Catching his attention, she whispered, "Who is that?"

He covered the mouthpiece and answered, "His name is O'Malley. He says Brady left messages for him to call this number."

Steve O'Malley. Joe's ex-partner. A man Joe trusted like a brother. "Let me talk to him," Annie said.

Her father handed her the phone, and she introduced herself. "Joe should be home soon," she said to O'Malley. "Keep trying his apartment. He's anxious to talk to you." She drew a breath. "There's something I just found out that he needs to know."

"Okay, I—" O'Malley sneezed. "Excuse me. I can't seem to get rid of this cold." He chuckled. "What kind of trouble has Joe gotten himself into this time?"

A chill raced up Annie's spine at the sound of O'Malley's voice, his laughter. She had heard them before. While hiding in the closet in Harry's office.

"Miss Macy? Are you there?"

Annie's stomach turned upside down. She drew a breath to steady her nerves. "Yes, I'm sorry. Something just came up and I have to go. Joe will explain everything." They exchanged goodbyes and Annie broke the connection.

"Honey, are you okay?" her father asked.

"I have to get a message to Joe."

"Didn't you just ask Detective O'Malley to do that?"

Annie punched in the number for long distance information. When directory assistance answered, she asked for Joe's home number, then tried it. "Oh, no." She glanced across at her father. "It's disconnected." She remembered the night at his apartment, Joe at his kitchen counter, shuffling through a stack of mail, commenting on the overdue bill, his muttered reminder to himself to pay it.

"Can't you call his cell phone?"

"It's dead. Besides, I don't know the number." Annie felt light-headed as she asked, "Can you fly us out of here today?"

"I don't see why not. What's going on?"

Annie reached for the phone book on the counter. "I'll explain on the way. Maybe Coleman or Nate can pick us up and take us to the airstrip. Then if I could just remember the name of the man Joe sent his mom to stay with, I could call her and ask how to get in touch with his cousin." Annie's mind raced as she looked for Coleman's number in the book. "The man she's staying with is a family friend, an ex-cop Joe's dad used to work with. Ed something."

Her father's brows shot up. "Simms?"

"That's it. How did you know?"

"He's the retired investigator who referred me to Brady, remember? I have his number in my cell phone."

Relief rushed through Annie. "Call him," she said, then punched in Coleman's number.

CHAPTER 15

The roads and visibility between Pinesborough and the city had cleared since Joe and Annie traveled the route together. He made it home in record time.

Mac greeted him the instant he stepped into his apartment. *"Just you and me tonight, pal,"* the parrot squawked.

"Looks like it might be just you and me forever, Mac." Joe exhaled a weary breath. "Damn that Dino. I thought I told him to pick you up."

He could see that his cousin had at least stopped by to give the parrot food and water. "Did you bad-mouth Dino, Mac? Is that why he left you to fend for yourself?"

Anxious to get in touch with O'Malley and tell him about the information on Landau's flash drive, Joe headed for the telephone. He was beginning to think Dino was on the right track when he had asked if Willis might be connected to the Emma Billings attack. But Joe hadn't yet sorted out in his mind how Willis might've pulled it off and wanted to hear O'Malley's take on that, since his partner had been there that night, as well.

When he didn't get a dial tone, Joe slammed down the telephone and cursed. He guessed he should be thankful the electricity and gas were still on, though he knew at any second those might go, too.

Joe walked across the hallway to his neighbor's apartment. Mrs. Bailey always seemed glad to help out in a crisis and today was no exception. Joe used her phone to try O'Malley and finally got an answer.

"Hey, Steve. It's me. You get my messages?"

"We just got home last night and I haven't had time to check 'em. What's up?"

"Can you break away for a while? I need to talk to you and I'd rather not do it over the phone. It's about the Billings incident. And a whole lot more."

"I'll be right over." O'Malley paused, then asked, "Are you okay?"

It occurred to Joe that if not for the sorry state of his relationship with Annie, his life would be just about perfect right now. The puzzle he had been trying for the past year to piece together was finally connecting. "I'm good," he said. "But if everything works out like I hope it does, I'm going to be a whole lot better than good real soon."

ANNIE COULDN'T SIT STILL. The flight had gone without a hitch. She had never liked flying in small planes, but she was too nervous over Joe walking into a trap to worry about anything else.

After landing, they'd taken a cab. She gripped the seat now, her heart pounding. Traffic was even worse than usual. "What day is it?" she asked her father. "I've lost track."

"December twenty-second."

She sat back. "With all that's been happening, I forgot about Christmas."

"You'll come home for the holiday, won't you?"

She thought of Joe and wondered how she would handle it if he got hurt, or worse. "We'll see," she said, turning to stare out the window.

Her father's hand covered hers. "He'll be okay. We made good time."

"And now we're losing it." She leaned forward and said to the driver, "Can't you move a little faster? It's an emergency."

"I'm doing my best, lady." The cabbie laid on the horn and cursed.

Annie sat back and prayed that Dino made it to Joe before O'Malley did.

"ONE THING STILL CONFUSES ME," Joe said to O'Malley. He turned on the computer in his living room, then returned to the kitchen while it booted up. "I think the attack on Emma Billings wasn't only intended to scare her not to testify, I think it was meant to shut me up, too. To get my badge lifted so I wouldn't dig deeper into the missing dope and money. If Willis did the deed and somehow got into the apartment while you two were out taking that walk, why weren't there any signs of the break-in? He didn't have a key."

Joe's mind drifted to that night. They split three shifts—he and O'Malley and Clayton Jones. Jones, having the most seniority, took 8:00 a.m. to 4:00 p.m., O'Malley had four to midnight, and Joe covered midnight to 8:00 a.m. There had been a light on in Emma Billings' bedroom when Joe arrived to take over. He and O'Malley saw it glowing beneath her door, heard soft music playing and her moving about the room.

As he always did if they knew she was awake, O'Malley had knocked to tell her the shift was changing. She was antsy about being guarded and had made it clear from the beginning that she wanted to be kept abreast of everything.

Miss Billings had answered O'Malley's knock by opening the door. Joe saw her from the next room and called out to greet her. Then O'Malley had left, and the next time Joe saw Emma Billings, she was a basket case and he had a bump on his head the size of a Manhattan high-rise.

Joe took O'Malley's empty coffee mug when he passed by the bar stool where his partner sat at the kitchen counter. With his back to O'Malley, he stood at the stove and poured a refill. "So what do you think, Steve? Any ideas?"

"I have a couple."

Joe sat the coffeepot down. "Oh, yeah? Shoot." He turned.

O'Malley stood at the other side of the counter, his revolver aimed at Joe, the muscle along his jawline jumping, his body trembling.

"On second thought, don't shoot," Joe said, trying to hold the coffee mug steady.

"Set the cup on the stove behind you," O'Malley said, his voice faltering.

Joe reached back and did as he was told. He felt sick and shocked and disappointed. Worried about O'Malley. Even more worried about himself.

"You should've butted out," Steve said. "I didn't want this to happen."

"Why me, Steve?"

"It was Willis's idea. He was wary of you from the start. He knew you'd worked undercover more than once to take down cops."

"Dirty cops," Joe corrected. "I didn't target anyone who didn't deserve it."

"You don't go after your own, Joe. You've said it yourself a hundred times. We're family. When you started sniffing around and reporting missing drugs from some of the busts, missing cash, that was it as far as Willis was concerned."

"I can't take down a bad cop, but the two of you can ruin a good one. Am I getting this straight, Steve?"

"I didn't want to do it, but by that time I was in too deep to dig my way out." O'Malley's face twisted. "It was either you or me. I'm sorry."

"You're sorry?" Joe made a sound of disbelief. "I don't understand how someone like you…" He shook his head. "I considered you a brother."

"Cathy was sick, you know that. I wanted the best for her. The best doctors, the best hospitals. The best doesn't come cheap."

Joe thought of O'Malley's wife, a once vital woman now ravaged by cancer. An honest woman. If her disease didn't kill her, finding out about this would.

O'Malley's revolver shook harder. "I didn't know Willis was going to hurt Emma Billings. I swear it, Joe. He was just supposed to threaten her, shake her up a little, explain what might happen if she testified against Reno." His Adam's apple shifted as he swallowed hard. "I knew you. I knew after the rumors got started, you wouldn't be able to work with people who didn't trust you. You'd quit and forget all about the missing dope and money. I was counting on that."

"I didn't forget, though. I guess you didn't know me so well, after all." Shaken by the sight of his best friend, his partner, holding a gun on him, Joe said, "Willis was there in her bedroom all along, wasn't he?"

O'Malley nodded.

"How did you know she would want to go out that night?"

"I suggested it. I figured she would jump at the chance. She was going stir-crazy locked up in that apartment. Willis hid in her room and waited there until after you came on and I left. I didn't think he'd hurt her. I swear it."

Joe took a step toward him. "We can work this out, Steve. Talk to me. How does Prine figure in?"

O'Malley flinched. "Stay back."

Across the room, Mac screeched and bristled his feathers.

"What's your plan, Steve? To take the flash drive?"

"I don't know, I—"

Joe shook his head. "It's over. Even if you kill me, Willis and Prine will talk. They've already named Landau. And I made a copy of the drive and left it with people who know what to do if anything happens to me."

O'Malley started to crumble. "I messed up, Joe. I really messed up this time."

Joe drew a long breath. Another. "Cathy will stand by you. I'll stand by you." He took another step, reached out. "Hand me the gun. It doesn't have to be this way."

"Stay back!"

Mac screeched. The cage rattled and the wire door fell open. A whirlwind of green feathers exploded into the room, surrounding O'Malley as he cried out and the gun went off.

Fire ripped through Joe's right thigh.

The apartment door burst open. Dino flew through the haze of swirling feathers and dove headfirst into O'Malley.

ANNIE RAN THROUGH the emergency room doors with her father on her heels. She stopped at the front window. "An ambulance just brought a man in with a gunshot wound," she said to the woman behind the glass. "Joe Brady. Is he here?"

Her voice was too loud, too shrill. People in the waiting room turned to stare. Annie didn't care. When she and her father arrived at Joe's apartment, they had seen an ambulance and police cars pulling away. A neighbor told her Joe had been shot.

"Just a moment," the nurse said. "I'll see what I can find out."

While Annie paced, two men who had been leaning against the wall by the door approached her father. "Mr. Macy?" the older of the two men said.

Her father turned. "Ed!" He glanced at Annie. "Honey, this is Ed Simms, the investigator I told you about."

"How is Joe?" Annie asked, and before Simms could answer, the younger man was at her side. Something about his appearance made her pause. The shape of his mouth, the slant of his smiling eyes. He was tall and reed-thin, with dusky skin and thinning dark hair.

He placed his hand on her arm. "I'm Dino Corelli, Joe's cousin. You must be Annie."

"Yes," she said, her voice emerging as little more than a squeak.

"Other than being half out of his mind worrying about you, Joe's doing okay."

She couldn't stop the tears. "He's okay?"

Dino grasped the hand she held out to him. "He took one in the leg, but Joe's tough as old leather. He'll survive."

"Were you there?"

He nodded. "Made it just in time to hear the gun go off." He frowned and shook his head. "I'd swear I latched Mac's cage after I fed him. If the door hadn't opened—" He laughed. "I've told Joe a hundred times he should clip the wings on that smart-mouthed pile of feathers."

Unsure what Joe's parrot had to do with anything, Annie squeezed Dino's hand. "If you'd been a second later…God, I can't stand to think about it."

"I don't think O'Malley meant to shoot Joe. That crazy bird made him freak."

"What happened to him?"

"O'Malley? He's in custody."

In custody. Joe's partner. His best friend. "How's Joe handling it?" Annie asked.

"Not good. He loved the guy like a brother, you know?"

Annie nodded, her throat too tight to speak.

"But he's more worked up about you than anything else," Dino added. "On account of you rushing here in your dad's plane and everything."

The nurse returned to the window. "Mr. Brady's with the doctor now. I'll let you know when—"

"Through here?" Annie interrupted, and before the woman could answer, she stepped over and tugged on the door handle. It was locked.

"Ma'am," the nurse said sternly. "You can't come back right now. I'll let you know when—"

The door opened suddenly and an orderly stepped through. Before it could close again, Annie slipped into the hallway."

"Ma'am!" The nurse started after her.

"Good luck trying to stop her," Annie heard her father say, followed by Dino's and Ed Simms' laughter.

Annie darted down the hallway ahead of the nurse, ignoring the woman's protests, peeking past curtains into examining rooms. And then a curtain opened and she saw him, propped up in bed, his face as gray as death.

"Joe!" She didn't take time to acknowledge the doctor as she entered the room and hurried to the side of his bed.

"Annie," Joe said, his voice groggy.

The nurse burst in behind her. "Ma'am, you—"

"It's okay," the doctor told her. "Let her stay a minute."

Annie cast a worried glance over her shoulder at the young man.

"He's had a shot of morphine," the doctor told her. "He's drunk as a skid row bum but he'll be fine."

Annie turned back to Joe.

"I'm sorry," Joe murmured groggily. "I'm a jerk." He wiped the tears from her cheeks, his fingers cold against her skin. "I need you, Annie."

She kissed his forehead, his cheeks, his lips, then laughed as she peered into his drug-hazed eyes. "I need you, too, Joe. No one else knows how to warm up my feet."

He managed a shaky, lopsided smile. "Wish I could help you with that right now, Sweet Tea. Afraid you'll have to catch me later." His eyelids drooped. "Definitely later."

Annie leaned down to his ear, whispered, "I love you, Joe."

One eye twitched. "Enough to take in Mac while I'm laid

up? Trust me, it gets lonely in that apartment by yourself. He's a good bird most of the time, no matter what Dino says."

Smiling, Annie glanced back at the doctor. "Are you sure he's drunk? I think maybe he's just using the morphine as an excuse to take advantage of my good nature."

The doctor laughed and left the room.

When she looked at Joe again, Annie noticed a flicker of pain in his eyes that no amount of morphine could dim.

"I'm sorry about O'Malley," she said.

"Me, too." He turned his head.

Annie covered his hand with hers, sensing he wasn't ready to talk about his partner. "I guess it won't be so bad having Mac keep me company until you're out of here," she said to change the subject. "But I do have one question. Do you ask so much of all the women in your life?"

A sob sounded behind Annie, and she looked back to see a pretty, petite elderly woman with gray-streaked dark hair enter the room. "He does ask a lot," the woman said, pausing at the foot of Joe's bed where she proceeded to burst into tears. "I clean his apartment, you know?"

Releasing Joe's hand, Annie approached the woman. "You must be Joe's mother."

"Yes." Dabbing at her eyes with a tissue, Mrs. Brady said, "My Joey, he's had a hard time this past year. Now this."

"The doctor says he'll be fine." She offered the older woman her hand. "I'm Anne Macy. Joe's told me wonderful things about you."

"And Dino's told me all about you." Mrs. Brady linked her fingers with Annie's and smiled through her tears. "He's a good boy, my Joey." She leaned closer and in a conspiratorial whisper, added, "But I warn you, he lives like a pig."

People were already leaving the cemetery when Annie's cab pulled up. After paying the driver, she climbed out and scanned the somber faces in the crowd. She had planned to be here for Joe, to stand beside him, to help him through what she knew would be a difficult ordeal. Cathy O'Malley had died three days before. Joe had been more than a little antsy about the funeral, about coming face-to-face with his ex-partner again for the first time since the shooting.

But just as Annie had been leaving her apartment, her attorney called, making her late.

She had not gone home to Georgia for Christmas. Instead, her family came to New York. Even if the police hadn't ordered her not to leave the city, she wouldn't have been able to go with Joe still in the hospital.

They spent Christmas Eve in his hospital room, she and her father, Aunt Tawney and Uncle Hank, and Aunt Tess. Joe's mother and Dino and Joe's aunt Sophie were there, too, as well as a stream of other Brady and Corelli relatives too numerous to count.

Yesterday, Joe was released from the hospital and they celebrated Christmas at his aunt Sophie's house. He had remained quiet and pensive throughout it all, and Annie had not been able to steal one minute alone with him to talk.

With her hands in the pockets of her coat, she made her way across the snow-patched cemetery grounds. Though the temperature remained brisk, the sun was out and the wind had stilled. She spotted Joe alongside a canopy, embracing a slender wisp of a girl. His gaze met hers and she knew instinctively that the young woman was Steve O'Malley's daughter Jayne, whom Joe had mentioned with fondness. After introductions were made and Annie expressed her condolences, she and Joe started off toward his car side by side.

He leaned on a cane, favoring his wounded leg as he walked. He wasn't supposed to be on it so soon, but she knew scolding him would do no good. In the past few days, she'd found out just how stubborn Joe could be.

"I'm sorry I missed the service, but it couldn't be helped," she told him. "I have some good news."

"I could use some right now."

Annie linked her arm through his. "I really hated not being here for you. I didn't see Steve. How did he hold up?"

"They didn't let him stick around long. He couldn't handle it, anyway. He fell apart. I think he believes the knowledge of what he did killed Cathy. I'm not sure I disagree." He shook his head, his voice strained and tired.

"If he'd come to me, I would've helped him out with the money. I could have if I'd stayed on the force."

"I wish I could promise that you'll make sense of this one day."

Joe exhaled a long, noisy breath as they stopped beside his car.

She took the keys from him, determined to drive, even if he put up a fight about it. "Why didn't you take a cab or have someone bring you? How in the world did you drive with your leg like that?"

"I did fine."

"Such a tough guy." At least on the surface, Annie thought. He was tender underneath.

"When you didn't show up," he said, leaning against the car, "I thought maybe you'd had a change of heart about us now that the doc says I'm out of the woods."

"You aren't getting rid of me that easily, Brady."

He frowned. "I don't have anything solid to offer in the way of a future. I'm an unemployed cop, I—"

"Here we go again." Annie whacked his chest. "If this 'I'm not good enough for you' routine is your way of trying to dump me, well you're not going to get away with it. I love you." She tilted her head to one side. "How do you feel about that?"

"It's just—" He cleared his throat, looked away briefly, then back at her. "I have a lot of baggage."

"I'm strong. I can help you unload it, if you'll let me."

He studied her, nodded across the street at a park. "Let's

walk. Over there where it's not so depressing. I have something I want to talk to you about."

"Your leg—"

"Is fine. Let's go."

She scowled at him. "Yes, Mr. Brady."

They crossed at the light. Once in the park, he draped one arm around her shoulders. "So what's your good news?"

"Are you trying to change the subject?"

"I'll get back to it."

She looked sideways at him. "My attorney called. That's why I was late. The D.A. is dropping my case."

Joe stopped beneath a tree and faced her. The sun filtered down through the branches. He closed his eyes briefly, and when he opened them again, she saw a hint of the old smile she loved. "That's not only good news, it's fantastic. Did he mention anything about Willis and Prine?"

She nodded. "No bail. They're stuck behind bars until the trial. Reno and Harry, too. I'm not looking forward to testifying."

"I am. And you're not leaving my sight until we do. The sooner we testify, the sooner we can put all of this behind us." With a sudden burst of laughter, he leaned his cane against the tree trunk, wrapped his arms around her and lifted her feet off the ground. "This deserves a celebration."

She smiled down at him. "Dinner?"

His eyes searched hers. "Since you said there's no getting rid of you, I was thinking more along the lines of a wedding."

Her heart stopped a moment, then started up again in double time. "Are you serious?"

He lowered her to the ground and laughed again. "Yeah, dead serious." Clearing his throat dramatically, he took both her hands in his. "Pretend I'm on my knees. I would be if not for this leg."

Everything around them seemed to fade into the background as she looked into Joe's eyes.

"Annie," he said, "I'm forty-one years old and you're the first woman I've ever been truly and deeply in love with."

Her eyes filled. "Truly?"

He nodded. "And deeply."

"That makes two of us."

"I thought you were forty?"

"You know what I meant."

Joe smiled. "Would you do me the honor of being my wife?"

An image flashed before her eyes. Giggling perimeno-pausal poodles in poofy pink dresses. Aunt Tawney fluttering around her, fussing and fidgeting with an itchy, crooked, delicate white veil.

"On one condition," Annie said. She winced. "Can we elope?"

He nodded.

Lifting onto her tiptoes, she threw her arms around his neck. "Then my answer is yes. *Yes! Yes! Yes!*"

His smile turned into a dazzling grin. "No doubts?"

"No doubts."

"You won't pull the runaway bride act on me?"

She shook her head. "Honey, I've been there, done that." They sealed the deal with a kiss, then Annie leaned back. "So where do we go from here?"

"What would you think about being a small-town sheriff's wife? I seem to recall Pinesborough County's in need of a new sheriff."

"Are you serious?" she asked again.

"You could get a job or go back to school at the college the next town over. Or, you could just stay home and be my love slave."

"Actually, I seem to recall that the women of Pinesborough are in need of a nice clothing boutique, too." She gave him a coy look. "I could bring a little Georgia style into town."

"You being a proper southern belle and all," he drawled.

She winked. "You mean a *tarnished* southern belle. Maybe that's what I'll call it. The Tarnished Belle. What do you think?"

His brows tugged together, and he poked out his lip. "I was really kind of hoping you'd go for the love slave suggestion."

"If the business goes belly-up, I'll keep that in mind." When Joe reached for his cane, she took hold of his other hand and they started off again. "We'll need someone to watch the baby while I work. At least until he or she is old enough to take with me to the boutique. You think your mom might like living in Pinesborough?"

"Baby?" Joe missed a step, stumbled a little.

"We could find her a little place to rent. You know, something with a yard and a garden like she's always wanted. And I'm sure Aunt Tess wouldn't mind us renting her barn until we can afford to buy a place." She drew closer to his side, murmured, "It has a great big bed we could get lost in every night."

"I remember." He blinked at her, his face pale. "Back to the baby. Are you trying to tell me something?"

"Wipe that panicked look off your face. I'm just trying to tell you that my biological clock is ticking. There's still time, but not much. I want a dark-haired little boy or girl that looks just like you."

"We can work on that." He stopped walking, tugged her against him, kissed her long and deep. Then he held her close, so close she felt his muscles trembling. "Does this mean we can throw away those little Christmas presents from Lacy?"

Annie smiled up at him. "I already did."

* * * * *

Turn the page for an exciting preview of
WHO CREAMED PEACHES, ANYWAY?,
the latest installment in Stevi Mittman's
LIFE ON LONG ISLAND CAN BE MURDER *series*.
Available in January 2008 from Harlequin NEXT.

"Setting the mood in your house is more than just a matter of furniture. Lighting and music can change your room from calm to wild, from funereal to party-ready. Baking bread says 'come on in.'"

—TipsFromTeddi.com

The parking lot outside L.I. Lanes, the bowling alley I just finished redecorating, is dark and cold. It's almost midnight and a couple of the streetlights are blinking furiously, trying to illuminate the parking area, but they aren't up to the job. As far as I can tell, there's no moon and no stars. Inside, there's a party going on to celebrate the "Grand Reopening," and the music is loud enough for me to still hate it out here. It's cold, I'm tired and I should just take my bow and, basking in the kudos, go home and crawl into my bed.

Only, there was this phone call...

Which is why I've raced out here to the icy parking lot after my on-again/off-again boyfriend, homicide detective Drew Scoones. I'm wearing ridiculously high heels that only an idiot or a hooker would wear in this weather. I must have been crazy letting my thirteen-year-old daughter, Dana, doll me up for this party so that Drew would realize how hot I am, so that he'd say, "Teddi, I want you and I'll accept you on your terms." These include not pressuring me into a second marriage mistake, accepting that my children have to come first and forgiving me the mother from hell.

That's what I'd like him to say. Only what he actually says is: "Damn it, Teddi! Let go of the car." He's using his I-am-the-police-and-you-must-obey-the-law voice. He should know better, but it looks like he expects me to just let go of the door handle and back away. This, even though the phone call I heard was from Hal Nelson, Drew's partner, calling about someone named Peaches Lipschitz possibly being murdered.

Sounds juicy, no? The phone call, I mean. Not Peaches.

Except for the couple of times when he thought he was rescuing me from the very jaws of death, I've never seen Drew so rattled. Rattled enough, I think, to actually pull out of the parking lot with me hanging on to the door handle of his little blue Mazda RX7 as he goes.

Discretion being the better part of valor, I let go. Heck, I've got the keys to my own car in my pocket, and how hard can it be to just follow Drew to this Peaches' place? As dark as it is, I'm pretty confident I can tail him without being noticed.

After all, I've learned from a master.

Him.

Maybe if it hadn't sounded like Peaches was dead. or maybe if it wasn't that Hal—who I really dislike intensely—appears to be involved. Then I could just let him go do his job and hear the details later. I mean, having redecorated the whole bowling alley-*cum*-billiards parlor, I wouldn't mind hanging around for a few compliments.

Only, the thing is, I've gotten pretty good at this detective stuff and I'm not missing out on this one.

Maybe Drew is right. Maybe I *am* becoming a homicide junkie. But examining my psyche while trying to tail Drew like a pro is probably not the best idea I've ever had. And, trust me on this, I've had some other *not best* ideas in my time. And my time starts way before my first client died and I met Drew. All the way back to Husband Number One. Now there was a really, really *not best* idea.

Anyway, thirty minutes and a trip down motive lane later, Drew pulls into the driveway of a well-kept two-story split-level in a nice neighborhood in New Hyde Park. I'm a half block behind him. I figure that's a safe enough distance for me to stop. I pull over to the curb and cut my engine. Drew gets out of his car and sends a glare in my direction that says I didn't fool him for a second, but that he doesn't have time to argue with me. Despite the dark and the fact that he's the length of an entire Costco aisle away from me, I can still see his frown.

When he's finally out of sight, I let myself out of my car, closing the door behind me. I do this as soundlessly as a six-year-old car will allow, which means that there is a bit of creaking. Actually, that may be my knees, since I've lowered myself behind my car just in case he steps back for a second look.

"Tire trouble?" a man's voice asks, and I jump, gasping as though whoever murdered Peaches is out to get me.

Which, since I'm outside her house, is not beyond the realm of possibility.

"Didn't mean to startle you," he says, crouching next to me and studying my tire before assuring me that it looks all right to him.

By now I'm standing up and stomping to keep warm, trying to look as if I'm more than capable of taking care of myself and anyone else who comes along. I make something up about how the tire was kind of thumping, but that he's absolutely right—it does look fine. I run my hands down my clothes to neaten them and realize I'm still in the Hooker Barbie getup—the same clothes my mother said made me look like a hooker housewife.

She'd said it in front of Drew just before he got the call from his partner, and he'd laughed. Then, after the call, he'd said something to the effect of I don't know how you Bayers do it. A housewife hooker. Isn't that what your mother just said?

If I was the type who put two and two together, which I am, I might put that comment and Peaches Lipschitz in the same sentence, and you know what I'd get?

Could Peaches Lipschitz be a hooker housewife? Or, make that could she have been?

The man beside me comes slowly to his feet, taking in every inch of me as he rises.

"You must be cold," he says, staring at me like I'm wearing even less than I am. "You, uh…?" He gestures toward the house in front of which I'm parked.

With as much dignity as I can muster, I tell him that actually I was going down the block, and I point my chin toward Peaches' house. The man smiles broadly. Too broadly, showing too many teeth of the better-to-eat-you-with-my-dear variety. "Let me walk you there," he says. "I happen to be—"

Instinct takes over. Some desire to protect Drew, if not Hal. To protect the integrity of the investigation… Oh, I *love* how that sounds. I decide that's exactly what I'm doing when I say, "Look, you seem like a nice man. Take my advice and go home to your wife." I'm protecting the integrity of the investigation.

The man stiffens, but his grip on my elbow doesn't loosen. He tells me he isn't married.

"Yeah," I say sarcastically. "And I'm not vice." I swear it just rolls off my tongue.

"No kidding," the man says, his hold on my elbow now painful. "I knew that right off. Wanna know how I knew?"

Sadly, I have an inkling. It's confirmed when he pulls out his badge and identifies himself. That happens just before he starts talking about arresting me.

When Kimberley Blackstone's father is
presumed dead, Kimberley is required to take
over the helm of Blackstone Diamonds. She
has to work closely with her ex, Ric Perrini, to
battle not only the press, but also the fierce
attraction still sizzling between them. Does Ric
feel the same...or is it the power her share of
Blackstone Diamonds will provide him as he
battles for boardroom supremacy.

Look for

VOWS &
A VENGEFUL GROOM
by
BRONWYN
JAMESON

Available January wherever you buy books

Executive Sue Ellen Carson was ordered by her boss
to undergo three weeks of wilderness training run
by retired USAF officer Joe Goodwin. She was there
to evaluate the program for federal funding approval.
But trading in power suits for combat fatigues was
hard enough—fighting off her feelings for Joe was
almost impossible....

Look for

RISKY BUSINESS

by

MERLINE
LOVELACE

Available January wherever you buy books

REQUEST YOUR FREE BOOKS!

2 FREE NOVELS PLUS 2 FREE GIFTS!

There's the life you planned. And there's what comes next.

NEXT07R

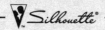

HARLEQUIN®

COMING NEXT MONTH

#99 RISKY BUSINESS • Merline Lovelace
For executive Sue Ellen Carson, approving or denying
funding for a camp for troubled teens is just another thing
to check off the to-do list from the comfort of her air-
conditioned office. Until her boss orders her to undergo
three weeks of wilderness training run by retired USAF
officer Joe Goodwin. Trading in power suits for combat
fatigues is hard enough—fighting off her feelings for Joe
is almost impossible....

**#100 MOTHERHOOD WITHOUT WARNING •
Tanya Michaels**
Della Carlisle has hit her stride with a great career, a
fantastic love life with a younger man, the works. But
one pregnancy test changes everything. The idea of having
Alexander DiRossi's baby and becoming his traditional
little housewife sends chills down Della's spine. It takes
her friends who have been there, done that, to make her
see that motherhood isn't the end of the fun—it's the
beginning!

HNCNM1207